novum **⤷** pro

CW00517407

Wolfgang Bader (Ed.)

novum #12

Volume 7

Great Stuff, Poetic,
thoughtful, meaningful.
liked P.73 – P.80
especially
Avid Reader

novum pro

Bibliographical data of the German National Library:

The German National Library records this publication in the German National Bibliography. Detailed bibliographical data are available at http://www.d-nb.de.

© 2022 novum publishing gmbh

ISBN 978-3-99131-774-6
Editing: Hugo Chandler, BA
Kathleen Moreira
Cover photo:
Volodymyr Martyniuk | Dreamstime.com

Cover design, layout & typesetting:
novum publishing
Internal illustrations:
see bibliography p. 163

The images provided by the authors have been printed in the highest possible quality.

www.novumpublishing.com

Table of contents

LADY OF THE NIGHT

An insomniac, Harold always went to the supermarket in the early hours of the morning. The early hours were a hellish time. Lying there mulling over things that would not particularly concern you in the daylight was a wholly negative pastime. He would make a coffee, get dressed and set out, taking a risk when passing underneath the tenebrous subway which led to the supermarket; fervently hoping that he would not encounter those unpleasant paid up members of the underworld who were inclined to inhabit and terrorise this graffiti ridden right of way at night.

Once out of the subway and strolling along the covered walk, the world became an overkill of rampant illumination: light everywhere. Scandalously sited on the beautiful river bank, the supermarket was a massive and garish icon of overwhelming bad taste. Some likened it to an oil refinery or a gargantuan interloper from outer space and you could easily envisage a disembodied, computerised voice booming forth from it and pronouncing the words 'We come in peace'; thus, encouraging the entire United States Army to blast hell out of it with every weapon at its disposal. Whatever, it was probably certain that only the lure of overwhelming 'money' and the promise of a new adjacent community and health centre that had 'persuaded' the purblind and completely uncultured council to approve its questionable construction.

First, the cash machine which, unlike the state of the art self-service checkouts, didn't ceaselessly harangue you and conducted your business with bland and dumb efficiency. No; even though he had a Welsh brother-in-law, he didn't want to do it in

Welsh. The city was not far from the border and whilst Harold liked most of the Welsh people he knew, he didn't like Owen, who kept his kid sister, Susan, short and treated her like dirt. Owen came from Abertillery and doing his best to help, Harold bought goods for her and his young nieces from the supermarket. She always protested at the time, but he knew it was a lifeline and felt he had to keep on doing it. He'd never married himself and didn't particularly want to; though it would sometimes be nice to have female company and he occasionally resorted to visiting a house of gratification in Meerschaum Wood which had so far survived detection and continued to offer solace to those who needed it.

"Excuse me sir, you left your card." A bruiser of a man, an assistant with close cropped hair and a prominent nose, politely retrieved it and handed it back to Harold.

"Thanks, I'm always doing that. I'll lose it altogether one day!"

The man surreptitiously placed a cigarette in his mouth, lit it and with a tentative smile, returned to gathering up and shoving the empty trolleys back in place. Only one door gave access to the foyer at night and as he passed into the main building, Harold studiously ignored the many stacks of bargains which surrounded him on all sides. Entering this vast secular cathedral, he briefly nodded at the mousey girl who ran the in-store pharmacy and directly ahead of him, the empty newsstand awaited the morning delivery.

Harold had never quite fathomed the layout of the place and often his quest for an obscure item would take him back to where he started. The aisles were long and confusing, but at this Godforsaken hour there were plenty of shelf packers about and feigning male helplessness, he found most of what he wanted without too much trouble. He bought things like tea and soft drinks for his nieces or tinned stuff like bake beans, all of which he knew would help eke out Susan's constricted budget. The trouble was that Owen drank and despite her having a part time cleaning job, there was no way Susan could survive without help. Harold was too timid to accost his brother-in-law about it, but he did everything he could and he knew Susan was grateful for his solicitude.

Quite satisfied with his purchases, Harold took his basket to the self-service check-outs. In the beginning he had sworn he would not patronise these relatively new devices but suppressing his Luddite tendencies which irrationally erupted over most things new and innovative, he had gradually succumbed and had to admit that he relished listening to the velvet tones of one checkout 'lady' in particular.

"Please remove an object from the bagging area."

That was his wallet. He'd put it down before trying to open the thin plastic bags. The bags were cussedly unresponsive, but he had found that by holding them either side and rubbing his hands together they would, with muttered oaths and perseverance, open up. (Eureka!).

"Please scan your first item." The voice sensuous, sultry and brooking no dissent.

"O.K., dear." The first one was one of those bargains with a yellow label and, inevitably, wouldn't scan.

"Please scan your first item." As far as Harold was concerned, she could say this in that sexy voice over and over again, but he supposed he'd better get a move on.

"OK, dear. I'm doing my best."

Eventually the reduced item did oblige and he managed to scan the rest of his purchases without difficulty. At this hour no-one else was using the checkouts and the skeletal staff were busy re-stocking, giving him, a strange feeling of isolation and he was startled when the smooth voice instructed him to "please finish and pay, please finish and pay."

He'd been daydreaming and awakening with a jolt; he finished the transaction and collected his change.

"I fancy you."

"I'm sorry, what's that?"

"I said I fancy you."

Strange what the night did. Illusory. Two assistants of equally large proportions and the compulsory dyed straw coloured hairdos were 'chopsin' not very far away and he thought he'd been hearing things.

"Please listen. I fancy you and I need your help."

The voice again. That unmistakable voice. It can only have come from the checkout, but he didn't believe it and if this went on he could see himself ending up in the mental health unit at the County Hospital. But what else could it be? He took the plunge; at the same time chastising himself for being a fool. He was compelled to answer.

"You need my help? What on earth can I do to help you, a disembodied voice? This is crazy."

"You must understand. I need my body back. Please believe me!"

"Your body? Now look, this is getting beyond a ..."

"You see, they took my voice ... "

"Oh, come now. Is this some kind of joke? I'm not on 'You've been framed', am I?"

This was becoming farcical and he picked up his shopping with the intention of departing. The garrulous assistants were still in full flow, but there was nothing to say that at any moment they would not notice his overly long stay at the checkout and become suspicious.

"Please don't go. I beg you. Help me!"

The velvet toned voice beseeched and he could not resist.

"What d'you want me to do and, for that matter, what in heaven's name can I do?"

"Please try to understand. They abducted me and my friend Diana from a disco and extracted our voices at the DESIRABLE TIMBRE OF ARTICULATION CLINIC."

"The w-w-what?"

"My body is still there and I desperately want to be re-united with it. Then you can have me. You can do what you like with me! But you must please help!"

Without even a backward glance, the assistants had moved elsewhere to do something else and now mandatorily enslaved by the voice, Harold remained rooted to the spot. He was now wholly intrigued and conjuring up, like any other healthy male, a vision of her in his mind, he came to the conclusion that anything he could do to help might indeed win him this desirable sounding 'Lady of the night.'

"But what-I mean-how can I possibly do what you ask? Your voice is-well- in there and your body …"

"Right underneath the checkout you'll find a hardly visible grey button. Get a bag and put it over the cash change chute by making a neck and a small round aperture. The, when I say, press the grey button with your hand, keep the left one steady and for Christ's sake, don't drop the bag!"

"Why on earth should I do that? You're not going to tell me … "

"Don't ask questions. Believe me, it'll work, it'll get my voice out! Please, just do it!"

Harold complied. He grabbed a bag, made a neck in it and fitted it over the cash chute.

"Now press the button and when you hear me say, quickly tie a knot in the bag!"

Tentatively and wondering why the medics hadn't come for him, Harold did as instructed. He pressed the button and, slightly muffled, the voice told him to do something he'd resisted for a long time. "Tie the knot," she said; which he did, partly because he'd fallen for her and partly because it appealed to his sense of humour.

"Now, let's go and be careful with me!"

Harold picked up both bags and almost ran from the supermarket. En route he passed the cigarette dependant trolley man, who was not possessed of enough savvy to wonder why this bizarre customer fled from the great entrepot with a full shopping bag in one hand and an empty, knotted one in the other.

Arriving breathlessly home to his one-bedroom flat over the local corner shop, Harold placed the bags down gently and with some consternation, addressed the knotted one.

"Are you all right in there? D'you need to breathe? Shall I open the bag?" It all came out in a breathless rush.

"No, please don't do that." The voice was anguished. "I must not be exposed until I have my body again. The fresh air would destroy me!"

To take a break in this surrealist scenario, Harold put the kettle on and busied himself with unpacking the shopping. "Don't suppose I could interest you in a cup of coffee?"

The voice did not seem to like this.

"Are you being facetious?"

"I'm sorry, but isn't that the classic chat up line before the steamy side of things?"

The voice laughed. A mellifluous chuckle. "Ha, ha! I can just see it in the local rag now. 'Man arrested for making love to plastic bag on playing fields! You'll have to wait 'til I get my body back, then we'll see!"

"And how d'you propose we achieve that and where is your body?"

"Still at the clinic."

"Still at the clinic? What clinic?"

There was a pause during which Harold wondered what thought processes were evolving inside the bag and what explanation the voice could possibly concoct. He began to think he was deluded and like a shrink might say, was just hearing things. But the voice was undaunted and had almost convinced him of her reality.

"They keep you there in a state of imprisonment and when they decide your voice has become worn and not fit for purpose;

they put it back or, if they don't deem you even worth keeping for other purposes, just dispose of you."

This was horrific and he really could not get his head round it. His doubts returned.

"Look, I just can't believe this … "

"Please don't let me down!" She began to weep.

"But what- I mean-how can I possibly do what you ask? Your voice is in there and even if I take you to this place, this clinic where your body is, there will probably be guards and … "

"Diana will help us."

"Diana?"

"I told you. They took her and me from the disco. She's my friend."

"She may be your friend, but how can she help? I don't see any way … "

"She was a 'sat nav' girl."

"A 'sat nav' girl?" This was degenerating into the absurd. It didn't add up for Harold, but having got this far, he figured he had no alternative but to go with the flow.

She became agitated again. "Please won't you just listen to me! Diana managed to escape and they caught her, but in their odd way they admired her and she now runs their brothel in Meerschaum Wood … "

"But how the hell can she help?"

"She knows people. There are people up Meerschaum Wood that can do these things."

"What things?"

"The voiceless ones in the clinic have their own cells. They sit around in the lounge all day but have to go to their cells at night. Diana was 'sprung' from her cell at night. They overlook a footpath which is unlit. It wasn't a difficult job."

"And Diana knows these people?"

"She knows everyone up there. She's now a poacher turned gamekeeper."

"And how did she find you again?"

"She shopped at the supermarket regularly and as there are only a dozen or so self-service checkouts, she hit on me eventually and recognised the voice."

Shall I wake up in a minute or maybe I need a drink, reasoned Harold.

"Will you excuse me for a moment? I need a drink."

"And why should I have to excuse you for that?"

"Booze is in the bedroom. I sometimes have a tipple. Don't sleep, you know."

"Can't do anything about that, I just told you."

Harold walked through the adjoining door and over to the window, noticing that a smear of light showed in the sky. Dawn already; the sun was still waking up at about half four and there were already one or two people and dogs inhabiting the playing fields by the river. He took out his mobile, dialled and a sleepy voice answered.

"'ello."

"I've got her."

"Good. You didn't believe me, did you?"

"Well, no, but could you blame me? Look, just tell me what to do. She's in the next room. She may be able to hear. I don't want to be too long."

"Bring her here at about ten. "

"What use will she be to them now? They won't put her back in a checkout, surely?"

"Don't worry, boy. They'll probably re-unite her and get her to work for me or somewhere like it. We'll go fifty-fifty on the deal. See you at ten." The line went dead and Harold fixed himself a whisky. He always kept a bottle on the bedside table and this was of more use than port in a storm. He made his way back to the sitting room and took the bottle with him.

"Who were you ringing?. I heard you talking to someone on your mobile. Who was it?" The voice was nervous, alarmed.

Harold decided to come clean. "Just a friend of yours."

"A friend of mine? How would you know any friends of mine? That's crazy!"

"Diana?"

The voice became hysterical. "You shit! So, this is a set up! And where did you meet her, you bastard?"

"You know what she does ... "

"Runs the brothel and they own the brothel?"

"What d'you think ... "

"Jesus, and she told you to keep using my checkout and you believed her?"

"I was intrigued, then you more or less convinced me with just your sensuous tones and quite naturally, being quite normal, I couldn't wait to meet the rest of you."

By now she'd recovered a little. "I shouldn't think there's much chance of that happening. Not now."

"On the contrary. She says they might even let me buy you. They won't accept you back in the checkout. They say the supermarket won't have second hand goods. It's too traumatic for you to do it, especially as you proved disloyal."

Anger took the upper hand.

"I wasn't fuckin' well disloyal! I was a captured slave. I didn't have any choice in the matter. The bastards!"

"Anyway, d'you think you might like me, if they'll let me have you?" This girl was subjected to big highs and lows and he could have sworn he saw the supermarket bag smile.

"Don't see I've much alternative. Possible curtains or working in a brothel or a good looking guy like you." Here she hesitated. "But what about you? As I said before, you don't know what I look like."

"Oh, but I do."

"How, that's not possible."

"But it is. You're a sumptuous redhead and I can certainly live with that."

"But how?" Surprise the prevailing tone.

"A photo. Diana gave it me."

"Not that sick one they took before they did their worst at the voice extraction clinic." Very audible disgust took over. "And I could never make out why the filthy minded swine made us strip for the business. What had that to do with it?"

"I cannot imagine."

She favoured him with another of her heart-warming chuckles. "Well, at least you know now exactly what you'll be getting!"

"I have to take you to Diana's at ten. Then we'll be off to Craven Arms."

"What on earth for?"

"To put your voice back where it belongs and to negotiate and with any luck you'll walk out of there not quite a free woman."

"And you can get this done in Craven Arms?"

"But of course. That's where the clinic is, isn't it?"

"I'd no idea where it was. I was never let out. And why would I be not quite free?"

"Because I'm your third option and you'd have to love honour and obey and I'll have to pay a lot of dosh for you."

Outright laughter. "Bollocks! And have you got a name by the way?"

"How stupid of me. It's Harold." Even more mirth from the bag, but not derisive.

"Well, I suppose you can't help that. Mine's Lucy and the other bits of me are called Lucy as well."

❧

An intelligent thug, Gavin lived in a nondescript house in Meerschaum Wood amidst all the other nondescript houses. He showed them to his car which already contained Diana, who was coming along to explain things. They'd rung the clinic to inform them they were on their way and the ghouls who ran the place affirmed that this would be all right and 'looked forward' to the encounter.

"It's quite a long way," said Gavin, "you'll have to be patient." His cultured tones belied his appearance and in a slight panic, Harold could not imagine what on earth a Voice Extraction Clinic might look like and why it should be in Craven Arms.

The journey took about three quarters of an hour and terminated, as promised, in the rather undistinguished town of Craven Arms; the chalk to Ludlow's historical and architecturally pleasing cheese. Craven Arms had one long thoroughfare and a string of mini-roundabouts and would not have been misplaced if situated in the lawless Wild West; meaning Tombstone, not Taunton.

A man of little conversation, Gavin pulled up at a long, low building just out of town on the A-49 and motioned for Harold and Diana to alight. He mounted the three or four steps to the front door and simply rang the bell. Above the door was a sign 'SOUTH SALOP PRODUCTS', a business which obviously acted as a front for the real goings on. The door opened and two compelling figures of Gavin's stature and mien confronted them. One took the knotted plastic bag off Harold and the other ushered them in with little ceremony and a slight hint of menace.

❦

A month or so later, Harold's brother-in-law, Owen, was driving over to the Cotswolds on business. He'd programmed his brand new Sat Nav and it was directing him to his destination with computerish zeal. It was funny, but he thought he sort of half recognised the measured tones of the male voice but couldn't quite place it and mentally shrugging that aside, his mind was invaded by thoughts of his missing brother-in-law. His brother-in-law had vanished some weeks ago and Susan was beside herself. The police had issued posters and interviewed people and even searched the banks of the Wye, but it had been all to no avail. Not that Owen cared much for the man. A bit of a do gooder and too interfering. Not to worry, he was sure they would find Harold soon and in the meantime there was little that Owen could do about it. So, he just complied with what the voice directed him to do and turned right, up the steep old road to Birdlip.

Stephen Constance. August. 2014.

A Collection of Poetry

Birth of a Thousand Years

Far away on the wings of hope and faith, there's a birth about
to happen.
There's more than that set before her, and she needs to find it.
She must find it. She should find it. She would find it.
Hoping. A birth longing to happen.

It's burning. Desiring.
It's knocking. Knowing.
Knocking on the doors of a heart, ever yielding, to the
discovering of truth. And to know.
Her unfakeable truth. Surrendering.

Where can she find it? Where will she find you?
Where are you? When? And to be set free.
Fearless heart. Hopeful. Intrepid. It begins to carve its way.
Far it goes, riding on the wings of hope and faith.

She yields to its majestic power. It's magical power.
The in-depth throbbing of dreams and desires.
Far It goes. Because it can only be far. To birth these glorious
tomorrows.
Near is too near. Far is perfect.

Far holds the right vessels that will unfurl its power.
It's majestic wings. In splendour.
And far. Faraway It goes.
To birth the Land of a new beginning.

The beginning of a thousand years.

Annotation
In this poem lies my story.

It's 10 a.m. It's breakfast time

The tears came streaming down again. Why do I cry about
this time every morning?
The gloom sets in as I sit on the chair in our dining room.
I'm about to have coffee, marmalade, butter, and toast.
Loads of semi bitter marmalade on the toast. Just the way I
like it.

My heart clenches like a fist and sinks. Why?
A sudden feeling of melancholy. Why?
I hear a whisper in the enclaves of my left breast. *Remember...*
My head lights up at that very moment and I remember.

Our days at the breakfast table every morning together at 10.
I feel you close. And then you say, this is the part you miss the
most.
This is the part I'll hold forever. I whisper back.
Come, sit, and let's have breakfast my love.

Take your seat at the head, like you did. And I'll sit at your
left. Like I'm doing now.
Tell me the stories and I'll laugh raucously, throwing my head
back like I used to.
Tell me, and I'll listen as I spoon cream into my coffee.
Stirring and whirling.

Tell me. My heart is listening.
My heart will listen to your whispers *forever*.

Annotation
For several months after the death of my husband. I felt a sudden downcast every morning at 10 a.m. For several months I'll begin to cry each morning at 10 a.m. without any visible or tangible reason. Even when I wasn't thinking about him. As I sat down to breakfast one of those teary mornings, I heard him whisper to me why I was feeling melancholy every day at 10. We usually had breakfast together at about this time and he was there to remind me that he misses that. Only then did I understand my moodiness at 10 a.m. every day. When I understood it, the emotions were replaced with sweet memories of our mornings together.

Falling is not failure

Falling is not failure.
It is the end of an era.
To prepare you for the rising of another era.

Annotation
We are caught up in what we see or perceive at the moment when situations become dour and we fall. We seldom remember that we are built for failure and to rise from it. We forget that we once flew and can rise and fly again, even higher than we did before.

Approach life cautiously and gracefully

When making life's choices, approach cautiously and
gracefully.
The choice you make today can make you or break you.

Choose your paths carefully and with wisdom.
If it doesn't feel right, walk away from it.

Walk away before it destroys you.
You may lose everything in staying.

And that, is a huge price to pay.
You'll look in the mirror and not know what, or who's staring
back at you.

Don't let that happen to you.
It is power to love you.

It is power to choose you first.
It is power to choose to live.

Annotation
So many times, life throws us off balance and most times due
to the choices we make. We get the inkling or that inner feeling when something is not right, and then we throw caution to
the wind and do it anyway, hoping that things will eventually
turn in our favour no matter what. The power of intuition is
a gift. That small still voice grows cold, silent, and eventually
we will stop hearing it whenever we choose to walk these dan-
gerous paths. The good news is we connect back with it when
we acknowledge it again, and in obedience. It will always be
there to guide us.

I will fly

You kill me *yet* again with your evil words, lies and hatred. I die yet *again* you reel.
I'm a prisoner of your evilness and narcissism. But only for a little *while* as usual, you see
I will rise and shine. Like I've always done. Flap my wings and fly into the yellow sun
And there I will give my light to the world.

The words you speak of me are cruel and filled with hatred. To break me, you see.
They are the prison walls you've built. To pull and to keep me down in your dreadful deceitful notion of me.
Yet, I remain strong. I shall rise because walls can only circle, but they can't hold me down.
The light within me, Love and hope will keep crushing those walls for eternity.

I will rise and fly into the beautiful light of the morning sun.
A butterfly with the wings of an eagle.
A star into a star I will go into the sun. It's scorching fire embracing my brilliance.
Your evil words only pull me down but can't hold me down.
Just like the sun chases the dark clouds away.
I shall rise again, and again. And fly I will.

Annotation
Like I have, have you had times when unkind, cruel words have been spoken about you which literally are lies to paint you black? I've been a victim repeatedly, in fact all my life, and I tell you it hurts raw – Especially when you can't go around correcting the lies that have been spoken about you to everyone around you. They will always have a distorted untrue perception of you. And

you can always immediately tell when you meet a person with a distorted view of you from the way they'll relate with you. I try to stay focused on the important things of life and in very many good ways have risen above these challenges.

Arthritis and Pay

Memba's Kitchen is hiring for kitchen staff the email says.
My heart aches. I'm worn. I cannot say
Crackling bones all day. The language of the bones cannot be concealed.
They don't wait for you to tell. They tell it themselves.

Finding no comfort. Tossed. Toiled to no avail.
I've lost strength to propel and to hail.
Still, there's a shining light deep within
Of what I know, I know in between.

Who can understand my woes on these days?
That I alone bear and carry through the throes.
I look around, and there's no one of heart to bear.
I'll continue to carry the part.

Head reeling from days and years of scorn.
Drained. Beaten. Bones broken and worn.
The pain I feel and bear alone
Who knows my days of pain and woe?

I plough through. The light within igniting an eternal fire.
I plough hard. Hope. Strive. With all I have I strike.
The know I know in between has come to stay

Too old to play and too young to wane.
Memba's kitchen's e-mail I will gladly put away.

What we know makes us who we are.
And that, we light up and become.
I don't want this email from Memba's Kitchen.
And so, I thrash it just like others alike.
Into the waiting recycle bin it goes

Memba's Kitchen just like others, offering average pay worn bones can't bear.
Memba's Kitchen just like others, offering average pay worn bones can't bear.

Annotation
I wrote this poem in the middle of unemployment and the pain of arthritis. It seemed I was only getting called for interviews on minimum wage paying jobs that were physically demanding. Roles I couldn't possibly carry out in my arthritic condition. Even though I was qualified, I wasn't getting responses for less physical roles and that was quite frustrating for me. It was a trying period of my life, and it birthed this poem.

A Collection of Poetry

Poems to describe the feelings of the child in the book "The Good, The bad and The Unwanted."

"A silent cry, a hungry child, emotions that were stunted,
When I was born, I was not bad but I know I was unwanted."

NOT BORN BAD

When I was born I was not bad, I sought for love and nurture
These are fundamental needs designed to shape my future,

I cried but no-one came to me, I sought for food and love
A tiny child left all alone where was the lord above,

And as I grew with no-one there to give me what I needed
I had bad thoughts, how could I not? this message should be heeded,

If I am good or I am bad it's down to how you act
You never threw a crumb of love, this forced me to react,

So, as I sit in my prison cell a child alone once more
If you are out there lost like me, you should have loved me more.

I HAVE A NAME

I have a name a lovely name, one thing you gave to me
A simple name a charming name for all the world to see,

And yet you never used my name as if it wasn't there
"The kid, the brat, the naughty child" I knew you did not care,

I have a name a lovely name well that's what others say
"That thing I bred... That bastard" was what I heard each day,

I have a name a lovely name but when the memories flood
I know you never echoed it, you must have known you should,

I have a name a lovely name and in my dark despair
I used my name to soothe myself as no one else was there,

Why did you call me Leo? I think you got it wrong
It stems from Latin origin' A lion... brave and strong',

I have a name a lovely name but I am not brave hearted
A child with no identity and then the beatings started,

I have a name a lovely name not used not in the least
No one sees the 'lion king' they see the 'angry beast',

I have a name a lovely name and dream about the day
That you might say it lovingly and wash the pain away.

I AM A CHILD

I am a child who was abused and struggled to survive
A punch bag often hurt and used but I am still alive,

I am a child who knew no love I cried but no-one came
I got no mercy from above but survived it all the same,

I am a child with nothing left with nothing more to give
There's only so much one can take and yet I choose to live,

There's other children worse than me some injured some left dead
I could have been the same as them but fought the odds instead,

I am a child who knew within a long, long time ago
I would survive despite you, until you let me go,

I am a child who learned to fight to savage and destroy
I used to be a quiet child the 'perfect' little boy,

I am a child who took revenge why bother being kind
"A vicious child, an angry child" that's how I am defined,

I am a child who was abused so many years ago
But no-one ever listened then and no-one's listening now.

I'LL MAKE YOU PAY

I'll make you pay you wait and see because nobody wanted me
It's not your fault but neither mine, another world... another
time,

Because I was not wanted, because I don't belong
I ended up in your cruel hands how can life be so wrong,

You try your best the best you can but you're a hard and
heartless man
You're not my family not my blood, you act the way you think
you should,

No-one's ever wanted me although you do pretend
You're doing what you're paid to do, I want this pain to end,

I'll make you pay as someone must for the rage that burns
inside
I'll tell them that you hurt me too and I had to run and hide,

I have no conscience anymore that's what the doctors said
I'll make you pay, you wait and see... I bet you end up dead.

A Collection of Poetry

GINGER THE KILLER CAT

"George I'm afraid I've got bad news," said receptionist Betty Bratt.
"Miss Johnson's just been on the phone about Ginger The Killer Cat.
She said that it's time to bring him for his annual booster jab,
so she's bringing him today. She just has to wait for a cab."
George turned a whiter shade of pale from the shock of just hearing that.
The pet that this vet least wanted to see was Ginger The Killer Cat.
People thought Ginger was lovely, so handsome, kind, laid back and chilled,
but they weren't the one that he hated. It was George who almost got killed.
Now vets have to take some chances. Not all pets are nice, George knew,
but Ginger took no prisoners when into the red mist he flew.
Miss Johnson arrived with Ginger, put his basket on to the table,
"Will you inject him Mr Purslow?" George said, "I will if I'm able."
Ginger looked quiet and peaceful, so George opened up the cage door
to find that his hand was bleeding from a slash from Ginger's claw
and then Ginger started fighting. George knew he had no chance to win.

Teeth and claws slashing and biting. Ginger's screams made an awful din.

George managed to pin Ginger down but that only made him madder.

He could not deliver a wound and so he emptied his bladder.

He flooded all of the table and George became totally soaked.

Trousers and shirt soaked in urine, caused by Ginger being provoked.

George could do nothing about it. No way could he relax his hand.

He needed both hands to pin Ginger. Nothing George could do but just stand

there holding the cat, so he yelled for Betty to come to his aid.

She'd have to give the injection while George just held Ginger and prayed.

Betty gave Ginger his vaccine, which wound the cat up even more.

George now had full on Battle Cat to somehow get through the cage door.

George knew that, whatever happened, he could not avoid getting hurt.

He flung Ginger at the basket, but Ginger got hold of his shirt.

Claws sank into George's shoulder. Teeth sank deep in George's arm.

George was getting a battering although he did his best to stay calm.

His hands and arms being shredded, George could do no more than let go.

Ginger flew round in victory. How to catch him George didn't know.

Ginger took off like a banshee, on cupboards and down on the floor,

but somehow George had to catch him and get him back
through the cage door.
George tried to grab him with towels, but Ginger was always
too quick.
George tried everything to catch him, but Ginger could foil
every trick.
Finally out of ideas, failed with everything that he'd tried,
George just gave up in frustration. He sat on the floor and
just cried.
Now Miss Johnson thought she knew better, put the basket
down on the floor.
Ginger, the cheeky old blighter, just calmly walked in
through the door.
Now safely shut in his basket he started to purr with delight,
getting some praise from his owner and laughing at George's
sad plight.
Now Miss Johnson started complaining about how George
handled the cat.
"You caused much distress for Ginger! I'm not really happy
with that!"
George was completely deflated. He could not take any more.
He stood in shock and disbelief, dripping urine and blood on
the floor.
Relieved when he heard Miss J's comment while on her way
out through the door,
"If that's how you will treat Ginger, you won't see us here any
more!"
George's spirits were uplifted by hearing Miss Johnson say
that.
He'd never more need to do battle with Ginger The Killer Cat.

I Had A Dream

I had a dream the other night, a dream that made me cry.
I dreamed man loved his fellow man. It made me wonder why
we find it so acceptable to have a world of hate.
A world of grabbing, not caring about other men's fate.
Where the poor get poorer and homeless forced onto the street.
A world where rich get richer while some have little to eat.
A world where all too often homeless are pushed out of sight.
Where politicians say victims probably caused their own plight.
A world with so much inequality, some might as well not exist.
Where anyone thought inferior, down at the bottom of the list
is made a second class citizen, a burden to us all,
with enough of our own problems. The weakest have to fall.
My dream was totally different. Man cares for his fellow man,
giving what's needed to the weakest, doing all he can.
No-one deemed a failure because we knew that he'd tried.
Anyone falling was carried. Carried high with pride.
No-one thought to be a burden. Everyone given a hand.
A hand of help and friendship to assist every man to stand
on his own two feet with success, safety and pride,
knowing assistance would be returned. No-one was going to hide
in the corner when their help was needed. All debts repaid
with gratitude and willingness. No-one ever afraid
of being thought inferior. No discrimination
based on gender, colour or creed. One united nation.
Gay, straight or transgender, male or female, young or old,
Christian, Moslem, Hindu or Jew welcomed into the fold.
A nation of variety not tolerated but welcome.
A nation that helped all its people, whatever the challenge or
outcome.
A nation where, if you cut one man, everyone would bleed.
With no intolerance, no despair, no want and no need.

I dreamed that God smiled at the creation Man had made,
a world that's filled with happiness, where no-one was afraid.
A social revolution had taken place with every man
helping to bring about the change, as I know we all can.
If only we had the nerve to make every man our brother
regardless of where he came from, his father or his mother.
If only we had passion and belief enough to try,
there's nothing we could not achieve if we set our standards
high.
Let love alone rule our world not fear, apathy or greed.
Let everyone be happy. Let every soul be freed.
I had a dream the other night, a dream that made me cry.
I dreamed of Love.

THE HOARDER

My life is causing me problems because I'm becoming a hoarder.
Collecting stuff is quite easy. Getting rid of it is harder.
I don't invite guests to my house. I'm embarrassed for them to see
the rubbish tip in which I live, where there is hardly room for me.
I've spent more than sixty years collecting all sorts of tat,
all stacked up, all over the place, with one chair for me and the cat.
Every room is now storage. Even the bathroom's now full.
Only room to reach the toilet, stand and give the handle a pull.
* Truth is that it all needs to go to the tip, not kept as a store,
to make room for me and the cat to live here in comfort once more.
I spent hours on my bedroom today and I finally found the floor.
Tomorrow will be hard. I'll try to move stuff that is blocking the door.
It's all just so time consuming, checking every item to see
if there's something I need to keep, something that's important to me.
So much of my life is in here, memories and keepsakes galore.
The trouble is, while I'm living, I'll keep collecting even more.
When I hunt through my collection, you wouldn't believe what I find,
artefacts of all shapes and sizes restoring the past in my mind.
Receipts from nineteen eighty-five, bills long paid and needed no more,
a thingamajig that's broken. I don't even know what it's for.

Photographs torn and disheveled, battered books with missing pages,
worn out shoes and threadbare blankets, tat handed down through the ages.
A broken cricket bat and ball. Perhaps the bat could be mended.
An oil painting that's scratched and scuffed if undamaged would look splendid.
* Could be a family heirloom that's valuable amongst the tat. There could be a hidden fortune just waiting for me and the cat.
* Starting to smell in that corner but it'll take years to get to it, let alone to find out what's rotting. Don't bother yet.
I could get more in by raising all piles by an extra three feet, as long as they don't fall over, as long as I can keep them neat.
I could stack some stuff on the bed. I could always sleep in the chair.
All I need is a small corner. I can't just get rid of what's there. It's really so overwhelming. * Would take a year for an army to clear out and clean up. * No chance for an old man who's gone barmy.

The Day The Earth Went Bang

The sun was blazing scarlet in the sky of impossible night,
while toxic smog bathed everything in iridescent green light.
An icy wind slashed like a knife through the oppressive
searing heat.
No-one attempted to escape. No-one ventured out on the street.
Land, sea and air melded in a wreckage of vapour and slurry.
Caused by man? Caused by God? Caused by nature? Much
too late to worry.
Screams of death, panic and terror from every corner rang
out in fear, horror and suffering on the day the earth went bang!

❧

Could catastrophe have been prevented? Something we'll
never know.
But plenty of warning signs were there when the cracks began
to show.
People who wanted to save the world were just too few in number
to be successful in their fight while warnings were still on amber.
Economics and ignorance meant the planet was pushed aside.
Those in power just made excuses, hid and never really tried.
Even red lights were never acted upon. Problems left to hang
until it was found to be too late, on the day the earth went bang!

❧

Governments showed no unity, planning or cooperation,
all just looking out for themselves, every parochial nation.
Big business controlled it all, accepting pollution for profit.
Finance was their only priority. No way they would change it.
NEW TECHNOLOGY would lead the way and save us all
in the end.

But technology costs money and so they still tried to pretend that they were KING OF THE CASTLE when alarm bells started to ring.
It was obvious they'd got it wrong on the day the earth went bang!

﹡

Can mankind ever recover from the hammer blow it received?
A new form of civilization with new ideas perceived.
A chance to build a new world based on cooperation and trust.
Not elitist but protecting the weak had to become a must.
A society based on sharing and love for our fellow man.
Maybe I'm dreaming but, if we believe we can do it, we can build a brave new world where, though depleted, HOPE, LOVE AND PEACE ARE KING,
rising phoenix-like from the ashes on the day the earth went bang!

Short story

THE COWARD

The guns! The bloody guns! All day long there's been constant artillery fire. Like the thunderstorm from hell but constantly, all day, without a break. We're used to it but today has been something extra. Today the bombardment has been even more intense, especially this afternoon. That's usually a sign that we are going to go over the top, an attack on the German trenches. Our artillery stepped things up in a big way around fifteen hundred hours, probably trying to take-out machine-gun posts and flatten the wire. Gerry responded a bit later, trying to spoil our preparations.

All afternoon there are constant comings and goings in the officers' bunker. Every officer must have been in there at some point, some several times. They're obviously planning something big. It has to be an attack. Everyone knows it but nobody wants to talk about it.

Around sixteen thirty hours our trench is hit by a gas attack. A great, dense, choking cloud of green chlorine gas rises and spreads through that section of the trench. Mayhem breaks out as men desperately panic and scramble to get away from the pungent poison. The sergeant, Sergeant Collbeck, is running around, blowing his whistle and yelling for men to put their gas masks on. Not everyone has a gas mask, but I am one of the lucky ones. I am only on the fringe of the gas but, even through my mask, the gas burns my nose and throat and sears my lungs. I stumble around half blind from the pain and tears in my squinting eyes, but I am one of the lucky ones. I don't need treatment other than plenty of water. We hear that six men were killed outright and at least a dozen others were taken away by the medics, but I am one of the lucky ones.

Things settle back to normal, at least as normal as they can be when an attack is imminent, but still those bloody guns continue. They have gone on for so long that I still hear them in my head even when they stop. At night I can't sleep because I still hear the pounding of the guns and if I do drop off, I have nightmares. Dreams of killing Germans. Young boys with sweethearts and mothers. Older men with wives and children. It's one thing to shoot a man, it's another to kill him up close with a bayonet when you can smell him, smell his fear and smell his blood. Dreams of comrades, mates riddled with machine gun bullets, their bodies strung up on the barbed wire or limbs blown off by exploding shells.

Everyone is afraid but nobody wants to admit it. It's all covered up by bravado and talk of what we are going to do to Gerry. I think we all need to get drunk, some Dutch courage, but that's not going to happen, so we have to make do with extra cigarettes and mugs of tea. A couple of the lads are busy drying their socks and powdering their feet. I don't think they'll be bothered about trench foot when they're strung up on the German wire. Some of the lads write letters home but not to post. We never know how many of the letters make it back home anyway. We certainly don't get many coming our way. But no, these letters are to give to a mate so, if he survives and you don't, he can get it to your family. We've still not been told about the attack, but we know. We all know!

At about twenty-one hundred hours the sergeant comes to us and tells us to get some sleep as we are going to attack the German trenches at daybreak. How do you sleep when you know that you and half of your mates could be dead in the morning? And still we hear the guns! The bloody guns! But now we are praying that they continue and do as much damage as possible to clear our way. I also pray for morning mist and fog to hide us from German snipers instead of the incessant rain of the last couple of days, turning no man's land into a quagmire and making it impossible to move easily.

I lie on my bed thinking about England, my family and friends who I might never see again. Whatever happens I hope they will be proud of me. I think about the whole circus that brought us here. The King's shilling. The blind optimism and patriotism. They said it would all be over by that first Christmas. Three years on and here we are with the end no closer. We came to fight Gerry and none of us know why. We have no idea what we are fighting for except some politicians told us Germany was England's enemy, so that makes Gerry our enemy. I suppose somebody must have a good reason for wanting us to fight. So much going round and round in my head. No chance of sleep. We might as well go now except it's too dark to see who we are killing. How many of us will still be alive this time tomorrow? How many Germans will we have killed and for what? Fifty yards of clinging, clawing mud, barbed wire and shell craters. Fifty yards that mean absolutely nothing towards ending the war.

I'm not afraid to die. I've been in this position before and been one of the lucky ones. One day my number will be up. One day a German sniper will have a bullet with my name on it. At least that's one way out of this bloody awful war, away from those bloody guns.

Around o-four hundred hours, Sergeant Collbeck wakes us all up. It's still dark but we have to be ready to go at first light. My prayer for fog fell on deaf ears. The moon and stars shine bright in a clear sky. I wonder if they'll be this bright tomorrow night and if I will still be here to see them. At least the rain has stopped.

Everybody is busy, checking their weapons, making sure they have enough ammo and sharpening their bayonets. Everybody tries to keep as busy as possible to try to take their minds off what is to come, only nothing can take your mind off it. No-one wants to go but everyone wants to get it over and done with.

The sky turns from black to grey and the order comes to fix bayonets. At o-six hundred hours, the order is given to go. Lieutenant Courtney and Sergeant Collbeck are the first up the ladder with much whistle blowing and shouts of "Come on lads! Follow me!" Everyone scrambles to be next, up the ladders and over the sandbags, into the open, away from the shelter of their trench. Gerry spots us immediately as we hear the sound of German machine guns and snipers. We are sitting ducks. It's like shooting fish in a barrel. The first wave of men are dropping like flies, cut down by the hail of bullets. The second wave fare a bit better. I am in the third wave. All trying to get across no man's land without getting killed, without getting blown to pieces, without getting ripped apart.

On my right a comrade becomes entangled on barbed wire that the artillery have missed. He struggles but can't get free before a hail of machine gun bullets solves his problem. He was a year younger than me, but his wife had a baby, a little boy, a month after he came out here. What a waste of life.

A mortar shell explodes close to me. Not close enough to injure me but it startles me enough to make me slip in the mud and fall to the ground. That's when I snap. That's when my nerve goes completely. I stay on the ground and curl up in a ball shaking, crying and praying that Gerry will finish me off. I'm not afraid of death but I can't kill anyone any more. I can't thrust my bayonet into another man's belly and see the look of terror in his eyes as he's left lying, bleeding to death with his guts spilling onto the ground. I'm not going to play their game any more. I lie there for what seems like an age, listening to the gunfire, screams and explosions, the sound of battle filling my head until I feel like my brain is going to burst. Vaguely I hear a distant cheer. I presume the lads, the survivors, have taken the trenches and put Gerry to flight.

We have won our miserable fifty yards of mud but at what cost and for what?

I stay where I am, still shaking and still sobbing. I am still there on the ground when the sergeant and the medics come to check the dead and the dying. Why couldn't Gerry have killed me when he had the chance? Why couldn't he have finished me off, put me out of my misery?

The sergeant finds me first. "Are you injured lad? What's happened to you?" He can see that I'm not wounded, no bleeding, no red badge of courage.

"No sarge. I'm OK." I mutter in a childlike voice, still shaking and sniffing back the tears.

"That's a pity lad. That means you're a coward. You've let down your comrades, those who fought when you didn't, and you've let down your country." He pulls out his revolver and marches me back to the trenches. God knows why he thinks he needs his revolver. There is no way that I am going to try to run. Where would I run to? Some other trench? Some other patch of mud? When we get to the trenches, I am incarcerated in one of the bunkers, with an armed guard, to await a court martial in the evening.

At around nineteen hundred hours I am marched to the officers' bunker. Three officers are present. The senior officer is Major Stanhope, the brigade commander. The other officers are Captain Worsley-Smythe and Lieutenant Courtney. As I am entitled to representation, Sergeant Collbeck has agreed to speak on my behalf. The officers sit in cold silence as the charge is read out of Cowardice On The Battlefield. The officers won't even look me in the eye, their faces showing their disgust and contempt. I don't know why they are bothering to hold the hearing as I am certain they have already made up their minds. They may as well just shoot me now. Sergeant Collbeck tells them how he found me lying unharmed on the ground after the battle.

"Are you a coward Private Jenkins?" asks the major.

"I'm not afraid to die for my country sir." I reply.

"Then why did you not join in the fight, with your brave comrades?"

"I could not face any more killing sir."

"Let me get this straight Jenkins. You expect us to believe that you are prepared to die for your country, but you are not prepared to kill your country's enemies. Is that correct?"

"That is correct sir."

"Permission to speak sir?" requests Sergeant Collbeck.

"Go ahead Sergeant," replies the major.

"The defendant has always been a good soldier in the past sir. One of the best. We've been in action together several times and he has always been in the forefront. Always been reliable. Never shown any sign of cowardice at all until today. I think something in him just snapped. I don't believe he had his full faculties sir."

"That is all very well Sergeant, but if more men behaved like that, we would lose this war. Your loyalty to your men is admirable but one rotten apple spoils the barrel. What would the men's morale be like if this sort of thing was not severely punished?"

The three officers go into a huddle, out of earshot, whispering and muttering. Finally they seem to have come to an agreement. I fear the worst.

"Private Jenkins we have come to our decision," says the major. "We have decided that you are guilty of cowardice, and you have let your comrades and your country down very badly. Such disgraceful conduct is unacceptable, and it is our decision that you will face a firing squad at o-nine hundred hours tomorrow."

I am taken back to the bunker which served as my cell earlier and again placed under armed guard. I am to be shot in the morning. I expected no less but still it comes as a shock. I Am To Be Shot In The Morning! My mind races, thinking of a thousand things at once and yet thinking of nothing. Nothing registers in my mind except I AM TO BE SHOT IN THE MORNING!

I request a pen and paper so that I can write a final letter home. I want to tell my parents my side of the story. They'll feel so ashamed when they get the official letter, from the army, telling them that their son was shot for cowardice. No doubt they will be ostracized and treated as pariahs by the neighbours. They are the parents of a coward! None of this is mum and dad's fault but they will be suffering all the same. I want to put things straight but however I try to phrase the letter in my head it still comes out as one thing. "Your son is a coward!" In the end I just write that I'm sorry, that I love them very much and that I hope they can forgive me for what I've done. I hand the letter to Sergeant Collbeck when he comes to see me. He will see that it gets posted back home. He apologises for having to arrest me but I had left him with no other alternative. I bare no malice towards him. He did what he had to do. So did the officers. But the words still echo in my head, "You Are A Coward!"

For another night I can't sleep. The guns are silent now but not in my head. In my head the barrage still continues. When I drift into sleep the nightmares come back. The killing, those being killed, the firing squad and still those words echo in my head, "YOU ARE A COWARD!"

At o-seven hundred hours the padre comes to see me. He asks me to pray with him, but I don't feel like praying to a god that allows all this to happen. Nevertheless the padre prays for my soul and gives me a blessing.

At o-eight hundred hours they bring me a large mug of tea and some breakfast, but I can't face it. I have no appetite and there is no point anyway.

At o-eight fifty hours the sergeant comes for me. "Time to go lad," is all he says but what else is there to say? I'm trying hard to hold it together and be as brave as I can for what I am about to face. We march a short distance away from the trenches to a small open area where a post had been erected. I am stood with my back to the post and my hands are tied behind it so that I can't try to run at the last second. Six men armed with rifles are stood in a row, under the command of Lieutenant Courtney. Three of them are mates of mine. They will feel almost as bad about this as I do but they have no option, they have a job to do.

Sergeant Collbeck asks me if I have a last request. I just ask him to make it quick. It's not bravado. It's because I am afraid, I'm losing my nerve. I'm offered a blindfold, but I decline. I want to look Lieutenant Courtney in the eyes when I am shot. I want him to see that I am no coward.

The order comes from the Lieutenant. "Ready."

I hear the clicks of the rifles as bullets are loaded into the firing chambers. I start to panic. Oh God this is really happening! I don't want to die! Oh God help me!

"Take aim!"

The rifles are all pointing at me. Oh no! Oh God! Oh God no!

"FIRE!"

War Child by Carole Leret

A war torn world
Rained down death from the skies
The night I was born,
Mingling the screams of the dying
and of those surviving
With the first cries
Of a new born child.

One and a half years later
The bombs came much closer
Without any warning,
Unprepared as we slept.

My parents calmly
Wrapped blankets around
Myself and my sister,
And carried us cautiously in the dark
To the top of the stairs.

My father a veteran of
The Great War
Just twenty odd years before
Knew something of the horrors
That now threatened us,
He had been discharged ill
After three years of trench hell
Shell shocked!
My mother too knew the horrors of war

Her youngest brother John
Aged just 19 or 20
Had been killed on the Somme.

This night of the bombing raid
We stood in darkness at the top of the stairs,
The roof was gone
The ceilings had caved in
There was dust and debris,
I can visualise it still
And we sat on the top stair and shuffled
Our way down.

We made it to safety
But not so our neighbours,
There were eight houses down
And eight houses in the street
Which ran parallel to ours
With no survivors.

Later that morning my parents
Went to assess the damage
My pram borrowed by a couple stood in the rubble
Their child silent now.

The roof of our house was restored
The ceilings rebuilt
New bedroom doors
A fresh lick of paint,
And after some nine months
Of being evacuated
We moved back in.

But death called again.
Days after our return my father died
And I stood by uncomprehending
As efforts were made to revive him.

Then birth followed death when six weeks later
My youngest sister was born,
And I took it very badly
With an outburst of anger and crying.
My aunts who were present
Said I was jealous,
Believing I suppose that I didn't understand.
They didn't mean to be unkind
They were just mentally blind
Unable to see
A little child's misery
Whose two years of life had
Known so much disruption
To say nothing of destruction
And who only weeks before had lost
Her daddy.

Only my mother filled with love and anguish
Put the baby to one side
And reached out her arms to me,
I had not been replaced
And so, I began slowly to accept and then
To love my little sister.

The war dragged on
The siren would sound
And the wardens with their mental helmets
Made their round
Knocking loudly on doors to make sure we had

Heard the alert,
And we made our way to the shelters.

The shelters of concrete and bricks
Were, we were assured, secure
Against a direct hit,
And I cannot remember
Anyone ever questioning it.

Our elders sat on wooden benches
Around the walls of the shelter,
And I suppose we children fell asleep
During the hours of the night
Until the 'All Clear'
When we stumbled out
Into the half light
And made our way home.

Then suddenly one day the war was over
And we had a big street party,
There were stalls and donkeys
for children to ride
And the young people formed a long chain
I remember
And danced and sang,
And there was joy and laughter
For a promised peace ever after –
But nobody told us children the bombs
Had not gone.

And one afternoon before I started school
I accompanied my mother to a matinee
At the pictures.

The News Reel showed the aftermath
Of war and there was the terrifying noise
Of bombs on the sound track,
It was all there on the big screen
And I slipped down to the floor
Between the rows of seats
And closed my eyes tight
And covered my ears
In a child's silent scream.

Yet children are resilient,
Soon we were making a playground
Of the 'bombed buildings' spaces in our street,
We played 'mothers and fathers'
Building our own small houses
And we found coloured glass red and green
Jewels! Rubies and Emeralds,
But diamonds had no value
Cheap as brass
They were just plain glass.

And every November we built a massive bonfire
And cremated the memories
Of the neighbours
Who had lived and loved
And perished there
Yesteryear.

One day while I was at school,
The bulldozers came and demolished the shelters
And the street looked empty and bereft,
But traces were left where they had stood.

I suppose they are now long gone
Covered up and forgotten
Along with the tears and fears and grief
All now buried deep beneath.
The Town Council eventually built houses
On the 'bombed buildings' in our street,
There was a wave of reconstruction
In our towns and cities
A recreation of our nation
To face the brave new war free world
We had won.

But wars are not done
Out there nor within us,
Down the years of my life
A sudden unexpected noise and I start
And jerk forward
A fear deep inside
The echo of bombs I heard as a child.

For we carry our childhoods with us
The sights, scents and sounds of things forgotten
Re-emerge and instantly carry us back
To moments in our past.

The sounds of war are like that,
The high pitched siren sending its warning across the town,
The merciless descent of a bomb,
The strange sound of gas cylinders
At the first warning
Releasing gas into pipes deep underground,
And the sound waited anxiously with accompanying fear
The welcome sound of the 'All Clear',
Allowing life to go on.

Sadly, wars go on too
As conflicts proliferate one after another,
Every new generation learns of a fresh invasion
Leading to a resented occupation
And children suffer the same
As families are moved around
Like pawns In a cruel war game.

We watch the effects on our television screens
Images that evoke anguish of scenes unforgettable,
A small boy sitting alone
Rigid as a statue
With a paralysed uncomprehending stare,
And the screams of an injured child
The sole survivor while her loved ones lie around her
Dead.

(It must be noticed that
We now dislike using the word 'dead' for death,
So, we fall back on euphemisms instead
To soften the impact of what is being said.

But words are empowering
Allowing us to say what we mean
And mean what we say,
Reducing their power by confusing their meaning
Gives a lie to reality.

So 'dead' and 'death' have become 'passed away'
As if 'death' is just dropping in for a fleeting visit
As it goes on its way.

The danger of lessening violence and trauma is there
Too, and concerning

For war with its accompanying brutality and pain
Should never be reduced
To a form of entertainment
In some simulated war game.)
The news on our television screen moves on
From traumatised children
To events closer to home,
But we are left feeling helpless
For what can we do about wars far away?
These traumatised children are not 'other'
They are of us
Members of our one human family
Our flesh and our blood –,
We send donations when requested
Blankets and warm clothing for the poor
Left starving,
We voice a protest,
Write to the papers and have our say
Or we contact politicians
For what good that will do
(Hundreds of thousands of us marched against
the invasion of Iraq – remember that?)

Have I aged into a cynic?
No, but I'm left with an impotent rage
Having learnt that the bombs have not gone
They have just moved on
A baton handed on
In some endless relay.

Then there are talks and discussions about defence
On keeping us safe,
And we unconsciously absorb information
On the construction of new weapons of mass destruction

The technology entailed, the ingenuity and skill
With their ever greater capacity to kill
God forgive!

Conflicts there will always be
Good versus ill,
An ethical fight for justice and human rights,
And it is rightful to lament the deaths and to honour those
Heroes who paid the ultimate price,
Making a noble sacrifice with their life,
For a world they would not live to see
Futures they would never know.

And yet
Peace must be top of the agenda,
And there must not be any surrender
To an avoidable war
The price is too high,
We must not cease to hope for a universal peace
A world free of war is worth longing and praying for.

But until then

Those who lead nations
Must be prevailed upon to never ignore,
That for little children there is no Just War
There is just war.

Anthology Collection

An easy walk

Along the canal
Enjoyed
Greenness and sunshine
Between Hebden Bridge and Mytholmroyd.

On this morning in May
With my water bottle and writing book
Picking choice words along the way
Then stopped
to write
Did not see the wilful stranger
Approach
In John Donne flea fashion
Carrying his armour
Did not feel
As the bastard inserted himself
Except later.

As Mr
Tick
dislodged himself
From its warm under dwelling
Between breast and bra
When I rolled out of bed
Heady and dizzy
Seeing for the first time

The red, angry mark below my left breast
Hearing the sound of a marble
On my bedroom floor boards
And I remembered that night
Removing my clothes
And though good reason to kill the bastard
Did not
Instead flung him out the window
to forget the intruder
and the exchange of blood and bacteria.

The End

Going up
Up through green fields bordered by fallen dry stone walls
Wood and wire fences
Holding in sheep and
Glacial rock
These are not mountains for skiing thrills
Only hills
And no snow on this spring day
Our picnic and conversation
Designed as an end to our time together
Interrupted by approaching cloud
The colour of burnt wood
And then droplets as the wind picks up
We packed up the remains of our picnic
Marched down the path adjacent a barbed wire fence
Marched past tangles of wool
Our timeline of shared memories
The sheep on the other side

Nonchalant
Unlike us
They warm in wool with lanolin rain protection.

But the trail down became a torrent
First a foot wide, then two, three, four
We slipped in the mud
No stable places for boots to hold fast
Only barbed wire to hold onto as our memories
Hurtfully disentangled
In contrast
to our amicable attempt for a planned exit.

Cold, wet, disappointed in the storm
Walking down
Down slippery slopes
No desire
To reach out to the other in the descending mist
Clinging and hovering around in wisps
Uncarded grey wool layered to form fog
In the valley below.

Heard a helicopter
Flashing light coming through the fog
Shouts
People surrounding us
Silver emergency blankets splashing blue light
Shrouding us
Keeping our individual body heat in
for welcomed warmth.

Got all clear
Emergency people off to flood victims.

We were rescued
But no, we, no us
The storm drama
Achieved the objective
The end
Of a relationship of ups and downs.

The Wonder of Parenting

Soda bread grows from dough so soft
After baking
Smells waft
Daughters rise
Wipe sleep from their eyes
The unfolding and stretching of limbs
Like plants about to blossom.

When did these young adults
Emerge
Whole, together
Confident in their own voice.

Each has a soliloquy of groundedness
And a gearing to fly.

Snowdrift

Bundles of sheep
Their dirty white
Adding tone and texture to the whiteness of the hills
Not straying into the ice encrusted
Snowdrift crevices
Finding the leeward side and huddling
Two black faces looking outwards to see us
Cuddling
Hugging for warmth if not love
No forgiveness on this cold day
For friends drifting away.

Not Coming Forward

I was told
She was not to be trusted
So, it was a serendipitous path through the undergrowth
Of work history and hearsay
Where other women were not sisters
And support a seemingly invisible commodity
Untradeable
The inevitable pronouncement prevailed
No evidence
For the injustice
Despite impregnation
of toxic words.

Studies of Forearms

The man at the front of the room
speaking assuredly
paused
meticulously rolled up one white sleeve
And then the other
Tanned forearms and black hairs.

With audience attention confirmed
He made his case for change.

The man in his home
Wearing his blue green T-shirt
Is washing dishes
Soap suds licking the auburn curls
Of his freckled forearms
And then on to the chopping of kindling
the occasional tense of a forearm muscle
Before wood splinters.
Another man in front of me
Sleeves rolled up like a tradesperson
Tattooed forearms
Strong hands, manicured nails
For strumming and picking
Fingers made for stretching
Sliding over the frets
Keeping pressure on the strings
To ensure the desired sound
Reverberating from walnut and sitka
A melancholic tune
Wistfully sung
Feeling his lump in the throat wishing
of past lovers
not to be.

Tea for One

The freshly brewed tea
Offered by me
Is a full cup
Sips not yet taken
No desire
For conversation
To visit someplace by the sea
Or anywhere for that matter
So why be with me
When you dream of someone else
with imagined pretence
Why be with me
When afterwards you roll over
Pick up the mobile
And check messages
Is she there or not
Petals from a daisy
Floating in the wind by her sea
You will think this is jealousy
It is not
And I am not fraught
It is only a phone
Helpful for mutual laughter or a moan
Getting used to being forgotten
Edited out of the conversation
No camaraderie for me
I can only wait
For someone to show special kindness to sate
The longing
Waiting for the attention I have shown you
I dare not
Confront

Your silence for
A well delivered touché
That even more silences me
Isolates me as past tense and blasé.

But I have worked at getting to know me
Knowing I am unique
A thinker, not part of a group or clique
Like a dancer
You cannot ignore
I have balance and a strong core
Capacity to hear your inner thoughts
With music in my ears
So, show me the door
If you will
But be careful
that there are no spills
my brew just may be a healthy antidote
for your ills.

Surgeon's Assistant

In her diminished form
Alice, the disinfected microbe
Wearing her sterile suit
Like a scuba diver
Complete with oxygen
Enough for the return journey
Plus, extra just in case
Settled herself
On the end of the surgical tube

And rode it from the appointed blood vessel
to that significant organ
Inside his body
Real and metaphoric
She had signed on to medically help repair the hole in the heart
of the man who needed to be loved
Genuinely, fully
Without emotional uncertainty
Her eyes adjusted
As she listened to his heart rhythms
She found the hole that should have healed naturally in childhood
Debris cluttered the entrance
Gingerly she stepped forward
The smell of blood unrelenting
Pulsating colours
Red, blue and purple multi-dimensional sculpture
First she removed an old coat
There were landscape prints in frames on the red floor of the cave
Then there were many photos lying about
Daughters and their mother, his family
an unsmiling couple whom she suspected were his parents
Did he look like his father?
This man of many talents
An old photo of a young woman with a baby's blanket
Looking like my German grandmother when she married
A boy at the beach, smiling
Beside a half built sandcastle
There – the beach bag that was in the photo
Then an odd assortment of artefacts
Discoloured toy soldiers
And a spitfire
Another photo, another boy

A piece of cake in a napkin
A Police gig ticket
She tenderly put the artefacts in the bag
And secured to the tube
Before closing off this forgotten space
With the surgical mesh sandwiched
Between hair cap and wetsuit hood
Flesh
would cover the mesh
Providing healing
Freedom to live and love
if only it was that easy
She slipped down the tube
Who knew what was in store for them?
If no air to breathe
If she died inside him
There would be no falling
Into each other's arms.

She smiled
She had reached the origin of the journey
Landing in the hands of the surgeon
Like a newborn
Becoming right sized again
And speaking of her remarkable journey
Without revealing new unspoken questions
How had he become the man he is today?
Maybe he had been loved as a child after all?
He who has lived through emotional pain
Lack of attention, limited affection
Seeing alcohol, anger
Hearing stories of crime
Hearing the silence
Of the family secret

Any love given or received
Overlaid and burdened by the obligations of others
Crushed under the weight of expectation
But he still craving.

Desire undiminished.

A Collection of Poetry

Avec Elle

Silencieuse et langoureuse
La nuit, qui voile le ciel.
Voleuse des rayons incandescents
Elle impose ses remplaçantes
Ses étoiles qui égayent avec gloire
Sa robe de velours noir
Protectrice, son rideau se ferme
Sur nos jours, un épiderme
Qui nous calme, nous apaise
Nos petits yeux, épuisés
Elle nous laisse sa signature
Invisible comme couverture
Depuis ma flamme cireuse
Sa douce présence berceuse
Penchée vers moi
Je cerne sa voix
Elle m'appelle
À la paix éternelle
Sous ma lumière abricotée
Je cède à sa poussière dorée
Je suis affaiblie
Depuis ma douce rêverie
Interdit de la voir
Je suis prise dans sa toile noire

CHATON

Et moi j'ai peur
Dans la lueur grise
D'une journée prise
Par ce temps
Qui sonne le début de la nuit
L'offrande du moment
Je lance un jeu
Avec mon chaton
Ma complice noire
Tout poilu tout pétillant
Il me fixe, son regard jaunâtre
Il prend plaisir à
M'examiner, m'analyser, m'envahir, m'interpeller
Me demander, me comprendre, me connaitre...

Et moi je ne sais pas
Et moi j'ai peur
D'une telle intimité.

That afternoon

Slowly.
Creakily.
Now I turn her face to the light,
her watered eyes
she plants in me,
as if to see
herself in me.
I share my with hers my young eyes
and feel her age.

Time sits weightily on her skin in stains.
Lines crossed over her smiles to seal in pains.

Purple-white fresh yellow pansies
In her bedside vase have no place in her space
Which breathes
No more.

The bath

Death stole away with her young eyes
To leave an eternal leaded gaze.
White on white, porcelain she lays
A china bride with sleeping skin.
She married her humid bed
Her choice.

Soft skeins of hair in dangled swirls
In weightless loops that drift and drown
Across her bones, ribbon around
Her waxy waist.
Redundant flesh.

Candy stick fingers turned to stone
Embalmed in ghosts of foamy soap
Yield to death's last fragile drop
She rests divine
Supine.

The Necklace

See them all, now they're fleeing
Cut loose, they scuttle fast
A polished sea of beetles
Swims wildly at my feet.

I watch the jewelled hailstorm
In helpless wonder
Their dance then stops in silence
All quiet, all gone, all released
From their captor.

I feel my empty skin
And touch my naked bones
My vanity their gaoler
My flesh a sorry yoke.

Their silver clasp has broken
Their task relinquished
Duty extinguished
Oh, how I covet their freedom
Their sweet escape!

To Music

I like to sit
and dangle
my legs into the water
and gazing up,
I search
amongst the leafy sky
to find I hope,
those two birds
who seem to like my presence.
They flutter and sit and they sing
to me, their public
And I then feel that
we have sung the same.

I lose myself,
enrapt by
this arcane choir.
Their canopy of green
a verdant summer stage.
I hope they know that
I share with them their secret Lieder
A sudden bolt of cruel wind,
the moment shatters ...

And then I feel that
we have lost the same.

A Collection of Poetry

On a random sunny afternoon, sometimes thoughts, ideas, musings from the past, present and future merge as you look skyward. The deepest blue sky and potent yellowy sun start to speak to you in rhyme. So, you close your eyes and respond in kind... maybe with something like this...

BLUE SKY THINKING

Sitting in the afternoon sun
I breathe deeply with heat on my back
Not a cloud my eyes can see
My pet dog lies strewn with comfort.

The trees sway this way and that
Their shadow cast spookily across my lawn
A small insect escapes the blades
As I watch it struggling to find a path.

To dream as I do
It only happens when the sky is eternally blue
A cool breeze refuses to share its energy
And supply me, my dog with sufficient air.

To feel my dreams, develop beyond
A horizon that is impossible to view
How the mind works to supply hope
To those who dare to dream
When sky becomes eternally blue
Radiating heat from the sun
Splatters on my face
On my back on my neck
It's the suns way of a loving embrace.

Yes I dream still of nothing
Into the eternal blue yonder
To find no answers as such
Light years from perdition
I hope and can only wonder.

Enjoying the reflective glare
Squinting with delight not derision
My blue sky that is above me;
Could it mean I'm looking; directly into the heavens?

A star; yes the celestial being
A yellow ball of sublime heat
And perfunctory light
I sit here to worship your power
With every bone and sinew.

The blue sky motivates the thinker
Metastasises the brain like an engine
Churns thoughts, hopes, the unseen shadow
Eyes open wide now as the truth
Waits for you unbidden.

T.O.W.N (The Overt Winter Night)

What does it mean when the temperature falls?
What does it mean when you are cold?
What does it mean
To the man
In the hall?
Does it mean
He is bold?
What does it
take to find
Heat? What
Does it take
To have flight?
What does it
Take to admit
Defeat? All it
Takes is an
Overt Winters
Night.

The Flight of Dance

Eyes transfixed, looking from the top down
Mesmerised as bodies intertwined
His with hers, hers with his
They were only of one mind.

        An expectant audience drew breath
        As her head hurtled towards the dance-floor
        A safe pair of arms and hands
        Could not deny her aura anymore.

Two turns, bodies completely in sync
Her hypnotic sweet odour consumed
For him to never let her go
As though they were the only two people in the room.

        She slid furtively across his back
        He spun on his toes to face
        Inches apart, hearts beating
        They drew closer, ready for their embrace.

Intensely their fingers interlock
Gripped by unbridled emotions
She leaps like a gazelle
It was poetry in motion.

The final curtain call arrives
Finely balanced like a bird on a beam
Did time fly palpably so fast?
And was this dance just another dream...

Homeless

We search high we search low
Our problems we own; confess
No need to put on a show
As we are the homeless.

How did we get here
Anyone hazard a guess?
We are normal; you have nothing to fear
But we are still homeless.

Out on the streets: this is our home
We try to make it our best
Finding the right place; takes time to roam
But there you have it: we're still homeless.

We locate the large shop front
Try to find warmth among the mess
When we roam we also hunt
There's no other way when you're homeless.

The light draws in anytime soon
Ready to face the cold night-time test
Sometimes when I look at the moon
It tells me 'your outside and your homeless'.

The boxes surround me as I snuggle in
I'm not a bird; but I'm in my own nest
I don't mind being near the bins
As I accept my status as being homeless.

In the morning hope reigns supreme
A Samaritan makes an offer: I say yes
On my withered, tired face a smile beams
Just maybe, I'll no longer be homeless.

I dream of this for everyone one I know
I speak from the heart; not in jest
We all need the help: tackled blow by blow
Maybe one day they'll be fewer of us homeless.

A very short story (drama/thriller)

A Dream Journey by Train

Samuel Peterson, a frantic, stubborn man, leapt forward in huge strides, as he targeted the 1615 from St. Pancras train station. The tannoyed voice ricocheted violently across the air, entering Peterson's ears presumptuously. A female high pitched tone droned on about the train he was about to catch, so he hoped. His legs moved swiftly now, like a greyhound chasing that ever moving plastic rabbit.

Sweating profusely, panting heavily, his thirteen stone out of shape body, lumbered towards the train, sitting noisily on platform 3. Entering the cabin, exhaling for a moment to draw breath, Peterson scanned the seats from his bespectacled view. Cabin H, first class, yes that's the one, seat number 13a. Fourteen pair of eyes drilled his. His stature. His demeanour. Decisions about Samuel permeated their minds. A tall, scruffy looking, male with no discernible instant appearance to determine his ancestry, perplexed the other passengers.

A large, untidy beard, covered his facial skin, as did his baseball cap on his head. An expensive pinstriped suit, finished off with white tatty trainers, sounded alarm bells in already prejudiced views. Without completely recoiling, as Peterson shifted towards his seat, eyes averted his as he drew near, as though Peterson was a storm or a hurricane heading in their direction. Then the moment of truth, seat 13a. There with her head down in 13b, sat a lady, about forty years old, auburn hair, glued to her electronic device. She didn't look up once, as Peterson, fumbled with his bag in the overhead space. He spied her, eying her over, from her head to her feet. Deliberately taking his time to address his bag, compensating for being intently watched by two men in seat 16a and b. This pragmatic opportunity delivered itself like a gift.

Finally slumping unceremoniously into his seat, Sarah White looked across at Peterson. 'Hello Sarah. We were wandering when we'd have this meeting. You know what I mean don't you?'

'Don't start Sammie. Drop the bullshit and give it to me straight for once.' Sarah fired back again turning to face the window she sat against.

'I'd love to give it to you straight, you know that right?' Peterson desperately wanted to smile, yet his professionalism didn't allow that sort of emotion or frivolity. His voice even, no discernible accent.

Sighing, shaking her head, Sarah White's beautiful, cosmetically manicured face, bright emotionless eyes, began losing some colour, vibrancy and sparkle.

'You lot better understand something,' she started, her voice low, yet determined. 'If anything happens to me...' Peterson and Sarah were interrupted by the attendant serving drinks. Peterson ordered two white tea's with one sugar.

'You were threatening something,' Peterson continued.

Sarah anxiously stirred her one sugared tea before responding.

'It doesn't matter anyway,' Sarah reacted sharply, sipping her tepid beverage. 'Your organisation will find out soon enough.'

'Umm I see,' Peterson, muttered to himself, something he rarely did. Then he turned to face Sarah, rather seductively, knowing she despised him and his intentions. 'My secret love, oh how my heart is saddened, as thou last journey on a train, leads to your final resting place'. His words faded as the sun does at around 8.40 p.m. in the summertime. Sarah's body relaxed, her eyes closing gently, settling into her seat, she drifted into a never ending cycle of sleep.

Peterson sat upright, nonchalant, calm, normal. Chirping could be heard from his right hand jacket pocket, the Mission Impossible theme tune by Lalo Schifrin. Peterson extracted his phone and answered.

'Is it done'?, was the question placed from the caller.

'What do you think?' Peterson bounced his rhetorical question at his caller. 'Of course, she's sleeping.'

That morning, Samuel Peterson, awoke snuggled up in bed with his wife Sarah, who didn't know about his murderous intentions to divorce her.

Machan Love

A Machan he is, in every sense of the word.
But not to me.
No, to me he is more than a Machan.
He's the reason I have life.
The reason and know what it feels like to be loved.
His hands are permanently perfumed with the smell of car oil
and he always carries around a screwdriver
and a tape measure.
That's what Machan's do.
They are ever ready to help.

To his friends he is devoted.
He puts them first, every time, before himself.
Being a Machan gives him so much joy.
And my Machan's love becomes evident
when he is with other Machans.
An energy amasses and nothing is impossible.
For the clink of glasses filled with single malt whiskeys
and the descent of trickling keys sounding upon the piano
fuel an endless bliss and right in those moments,
dreams are conjured up.
Like rice bubbling away whilst cooking atop a stove.
His genius is obvious,
as is his unfulfilled potential.
He's a Machan who prefers to wear builder's trousers,
covered in paint
and always dons a baseball cap to hide his balding.

He would have been a millionaire,
had he not given all of his money to others, but...
That's what Machan's do.
They are ever ready to give.

I remember when my Machan built a house
with a blanket and four chairs.
I wanted to live in it forever.
He would invite other Machans to come and have air tea
and air sandwiches with us.
Life was simple and wonderful.
But as I grew, so did my Machan's weariness.
The creases in his smile lines deepened
but so did the creases in his worry lines.
Even so, he was never caught without a smile on his face.
Machan once built me a swing made of crochet rope
and tied it to the roof of an outside veranda.
'Push me again Machan!', I would shout, standing up in it,
as I swung without a care in the world.
But Machan got onto my swing to have a turn himself
and the whole roof came crashing down on top of him.
Still smiling and covered in roof,
he said he'd build me another one.
That's what Machan's do.
They are ever ready to keep a promise.

Machan built me many things over the years
including a poruwa on my wedding day.
A sentimental Machan,
he used parts of my baby cot and first toys that he had kept
to make the intricate decorations upon it.
More promises were made when he became a grand-Machan
including the time he put little man into a holdall bag,
zipped him up to his neck

and swung him by the handles round the room
so he felt like he was on a roller coaster.
He also dragged big girl around the kitchen by her legs
so that she could pretend she was
a choo-choo train,
snaking about the house.
Baby girl loved to watch Machan
tiling the patio from the window too
and would talk to him the whole time while he worked.
Machan knew all of the special baby words
with which to reply.
That's what Machan's do
They are ever ready to learn baby language.

'Hello Machan,' everyone greeted him.
And there, with a smile, Machan would be,
whatever time of day, ever ready.
But we were not.
I was not. It was not his time.
Machan always gets better.
'Remember that time he fell two storeys from a ladder
and drove himself home with a dislocated shoulder?'
Machan is indestructible.
He will be fine.
'He's being taken to hospital,' we were told.
'His oxygen levels are low.'
I was my Machan's Machan,
but he had other Machan's like me, my brother Machan's
and the grand-Machan's too,
not to forget the Machan's of his generation,
lifelong Machan's.
None of us knew what to do.
None of us were ready.
Up and down the holdall bag-less roller coaster ran.
For weeks, Machan showed his genius fighting spirit.

But Machan couldn't do what Machan's do.
His screwdriver and measuring tape, not in hand,
Machan was defenceless.
When the doctors called us from the hospital
and asked us to come in,
we knew it was time to say our goodbyes to Machan.
It was time to put our sadness to one side.
That's what Machan's do
They are ever ready to put others before themselves.

We cloaked ourselves in hospital gowns, gloves and masks
and entered the stark and lifeless hospital side room.
Unable to touch Machan's skin or kiss his cheek
as he had done for us for years,
we stroked Machan's head with gloved hands,
feeling the warmth penetrate through the rubber
that separated us.
We told him that he was the best Machan
anyone could have ever wished for.
And washed Machan's baseball cap-less balding head
with holy water and prayed for him.
Tears streamed down our cheeks
but we did not allow ourselves to choke up as we said
the holy words over his still body.
As the last word of the prayer was spoken,
The machines connected to Machan all started to beep.
Machan had waited for us to come and see him one last time
before deciding to leave.
That's what Machan's do.
They are ever ready to wait for the perfect timing.

As the news of Machan's passing,
reached all of the other Machan's he knew,
an outpouring of Machan love ensued.

Never had it been known
just how much of a Machan he had been.
Giving driving lessons to his Machan's children.
Driving for hours
to help a Machan who was locked out of their home.
Holding a number of Machan's hands
as they lost their husbands, wives and children.
Building a house for a Machan.
Selling his belongings
to help raise money for a Machan in need.
The examples of Machan's love were abundant and endless.
And we all still share stories about Machan.
Machan love.
There's nothing like it.
We know you are still here with us Machan.
That's why we still talk to you.
That's what Machan's do.
They are ever ready to give Machan love.

Jim's Jingles

Our Friend Jim

We have a friend called Jim,
Who has us all befuddled,
He told us he's a hard man,
But then likes to be cuddled.

Pricey was a fighter,
By all accounts a thug,
But nor it seems no happier
Than when he got a hug.

He's turned into a poet,
His sonnets are insightful
And when he has his dancing shoes
His tapping is delightful.

But really there's no mystery,
It's Jesus he embraces,
And now this big old softie
Puts a smile on all our faces.

Mjr. Michelle Hugging
(Salvation Army, 2013)

Courting!

I once courted a German girl,
Her brother's name was Roland,
It wasn't meant to last for I was quite aghast!
When she kept wanting to invade Poland.
Then when I met Lil, I was instantly cheered,
Things were going well, till she grew a long beard!
I must just appeal to you Care Staff,
When you come over here for a fag,
Don't introduce me to someone,
Looking like Les Dawson in drag!

Ode to Carers

Actors learn lines which they then repeat.
Rock stars sing songs and we tap our feet.
In other words, they entertain,
Whilst you our very lives maintain!
Entertainers do not wash, feed, dress.
I'm sure they'd make a right old mess!

So why is an entertainer made a Knight?
Not someone like you! That's not right!
Ask someone who's dying or sick:
If they need Sir David or Sir Mick (Jagger).
Even if it's something less serious like flu,
The person most needed, without doubt is you!

No wonder we get all anxious and tense
For what on earth has happened, to good old common sense.
For if I catch a burglar pinching my stuff,
I'll be in deep trouble if he's hurt if I get rough!
And if Alfie misbehaves in school, and teacher puts him
right,
Mummy's at the school gate, looking for a fight.
And little mixed up Percy, has caused such deep distress.
He's been told he can't attend school in his sisters Sunday
dress!
So be careful what you say to someone sensitive to slights,
Or you'll end up in the courtroom because they know their
rights!

'Time' (Friend or Enemy?)

Why have I tried to cultivate a certain charm and wit?
It's due to time transforming me into an ugly old git!
We are all in fact victims of something we call time.
A word that's only virtue is it's dead easy to rhyme.
It's the ladies who I pity. Who started life as pretty.
But now life is a drag. They've become an ancient fag.
Their femininity has disappeared. They're like Les Dawson in drag!
And if that's not enough, far apart from looking rough.
Your memory starts to go, like dear old Uncle Jo.
So, forgive me if I forget your name. Short time memory is to blame!
Many other health problems have come to the fore.
But I won't become a bloody bore.
There's one source of comfort I must mention. For we have a third dimension.
Although these things will never cease, my faith in God brings me peace!
And despite the aforementioned, from one once super fit,
I never ever will become a miserable old git!
I've great respect for all your staff.
Please join me in a bloody good laugh.

Extract from his book
'Murdering the Macho Managers'

Latency

Having set the scene clearly in the minds of all employees that life was not going to be a picnic I settled into a working pattern. The usual bread and butter stuff of recruitment, selection, terms and conditions of appointment, payroll, training, systems development and the like.

I made it very clear that I was a consultant with professional standards. I am, and I will be seen to be proficient in the business of people management. I deliver effective people strategies. I also ensure that I am seen as highly committed to ethical standards. I also make it clear that I can apply and adapt techniques for people management to fit the needs of organisations and the people who work in them. There are times when I use the first person singular as an icon.

I let it be known that I am highly skilled in the management of change and am personally committed to my continuing professional development. A cursory glance at some of the older, fatter personnel files did show that a certain consistency of approach was seriously needed.

Sarah had worked in the firm a very long time.

When she joined employment well before the old days of Dr Strauski she had the compound disadvantages of being a woman at work and being black. Time went by and a further disadvantage was apparent in that, whilst at work, she became disabled.

Some weeks before viewing Sarah's file I took a day off work and went to visit some friends of mine.

They were staying down at the Stables by Camden Lock. If you worked for the Local Authority there you could visit them for free at the time. A mixed race couple they successfully travelled around the country talking of their lives and the adversities they faced along the way. Their names were Anne Frank and Steven Lawrence.

Stephen and Anne are a great couple. They spent their time travelling around the country teaching people who would listen and care about what happens in places where the workforce isn't managed governed or financed properly and therefore neither is society. Stephen and Anne are separated by time and space. Stephen was born in Jamaica in the early seventies whilst Anne was born in Germany in the late twenties.

Both of them had a lot going for them. Stephen was a cub and then an accomplished boy scout.

Not only had he taken part in the London Greenwich mini marathon, but the sweatshirt he completed the race in is there for all to see.

Stephen was a handsome young man. To-day he could be working in London. He'd probably be working miracles in London like many of the young gifted and black kids are doing to-day. But he was brutally murdered by mindless animals on 22nd April 1993. Nelson Mandela has reminded us that "... the Laurence's tragedy is our tragedy." Stephen is working miracles despite his brutal murder side by side with Anne.

Anne was a beautiful and talented young girl in her day. Before she and her family went underground, she was bright and chatty. She quickly made friends at school. Anne was envied by many of her generation. Both she and her family had somewhere to hide from the Nazi's. She took her diary with her and some old letters. Then she added curlers, handkerchiefs and a comb. Otto Frank and his beautiful wife kept their family and four other fugitives together and safe until capture in 1944. Anne's diary is one of the most read nonfiction books in the world.

The message of the Anne and Stephen exhibition reminds us that the future is really in the hands of each of us as individuals. The choices we make will determine tomorrow's history. Essentially the message is one of youth and hope. Anne wrote a diary, Stephen ran a marathon. Where there is youth there is hope, freedom and creativity.

Reading through Sarah's file, and then spending hours more re-reading the file in disbelief, soon draws any youth, hope or creativity out of any personnel officer I have shown it to, even to this day.

Her file was remarkable from the very first line of her contract of employment. She was actually employed by the factory that had preceded Strauski's move into the building.

She came to the organisation along with assets such as rusted filing cabinets in the basement and compound and complex encyclopedism of a Human Resources employment law practitioner.

The old firm were happy to hand her over unannounced with the fixtures and fittings as a transfer of undertaking along with a job lot. Why? I read on.

In the early eighties Sally had been employed as a trainee. Her father was good friends with the owner of the firm, she had not been given a fair chance at City and Guilds. Reading between the lines, the last two statements above were probably false.

A Collection of Poetry

Another Man

She lives with another man now, no longer here with me;
he doesn't speak the language, it's better that way you see.
I told her that I loved her, but she didn't want to know
she played on all my heartstrings, there on my shirtsleeve
shown.

I would always take her back again, without a second
thought;
the lass that speaks when spoken to, with ne'er e'en one retort.
They only live across the street; I watch them walk on by,
strolling arm in arm complete, I can only sigh.

So, in the past shaken senseless; she'd been raped and beat
mocked and scorned and petrified, then a refuge her home
complete.
She doesn't like to talk much, after all that she's been
through;
betrayal, abuse and bullying, she's had enough of that it's true.

JELL AND TARR

A FOLKTALE OF WARNING TO ANY NUCLEAR
FAMILIES WHO MAY HAVE SURVIVED.

Chapter 1

Two owls were there that were born out of bat trees separate,
but whose night loops cast them farther afield than their cousins.
(The bats).
Their meeting was a coupling and their coupling named them.
More owlish names there are not than those of Jell and Tarr.
Needless to say, they flew well and far.

More swift than chimps were the splicings of mice's behinds
that kept them full fat fed.

"Efficiency", it should be said,
"Is not a word well spelt in owl vocabulary,"
But in this way Jell and Tarr prospered.
Out of the Sun, sometime there must come
a manifestation of the potential, a kinetic monster
that for all senses and purposes must be named
DANGEROUSE.
This monster has eyes of lead, this monster has claws of black steal.
(Sinewy talons to match) downy wings dragged from dragon's
backs
are strapped to the engine that slams downs from further
than Heafonum.
Death sits on the peak of the deadly beak of Eagle.

Eagle is daylight death. Colder than space itself
and more accurate than time.
It was in this way that Eagle prospered.

"Happiness" it should be said, "is not a word well spelt in owl vocabulary,"
but nestling content, a good many mice masticated
secure enough to sleep, side by side, with only wings pressed together
Jell and Tarr slept, ill hidden from the rising sun.

Chapter 2

The bright lemon eye rose, and with it Eagle.
Quicker than the razored air through which Eagle shot
that homed Eagle's destination from a light year at least
the tawny treachery of Jell's feathers.

Jell and Tarr slept. There was no reason,
no warning bell from Heaven to prick them awake.
Eagle was wound, held in the air,
a mile above, held in the air a mile above and in front of The Sun.
Ten seconds would suffice!

Eagle has come, Eagle was come, Eagle had come.

There was no reason there was no call
for Tarr to rise as she did, screeching,
a hundred yards high in an instant
to meet the thunderous Eagle's fall.

Jell awoke and saw Tarr insensible, a wing disjointed
a bloody face, but cradled firm, in the greenest tree recoverable.
Then Jell saw the end of Eagle's flight.
Tarr's unwarranted interception meant impalement

on an upturned sharpened branch. Intestines now that
hugged the tree
almost independently. neck craning, talons searching for a
land hold
not to be found. Bloody eyes wandering in sockets soon to be
hollowed.
A spoiled machine foundered too far from home.

"Thank goodness" it should be said, "is not a word well spelt
in owl vocabulary,"
but anyway
Tarr's green cradle heralded sweet, sweet spring.

Chapter 3

If wounds are healed by time, then callouses as well do grow
on body and on mind.
Further in the year we see Jell and Tarr with a new found
security
that shall be called Child.
Although the birth could not be faulted, it bore of itself
the unwarranted pride called Family.
Jell and Tarr were satisfied.

Not far away at crow's speed, there lay a goodly peopled
village (called Leeds)
that was terrorised by a dragon (called dragon)
who carried away the children and ate them.
The cry spread the future was at stake.

The cry spread, dragon had to be taken
For the children's sake.
Up pricked the ears of Jell and Tarr. They heard the news, the
duty was theirs.

They killed the Eagle, now they must be dragon slayer's both
not heading the ominous change in goalposts!

Dawn

The town knelt down for Jell and Tarr, who waited alert to
face their facer
the rampant savage dragon.

If you have never seen an English hill
that sits like a big green roll to flop
invisible over the horizon
then never try so size dragon
If you have never stared at that convex blue egg called sky or
Heafonum
then never try to imagine the concave breast of dragon.
If you have never seen the size or light of cold blue moon full
then never gaze into dragon's eyes.
Jell and Tarr, they wait erect
their family and town they must protect.

Dragon did not so much come as rise over the horizon.
Cold blue orbs for eyes and breathing smoke, then fire.
"Heroism" it should be said, "is not a word that is well spelt in
owl vocabulary,"
but to the town, both Jell and Tarr are well and truly heroes
now.

Dragon comes hard on faster than a meteorite mass
to crush the family group called owl.
Jell is up, his feather's out to fly into the mouth of dragon
and choke the scourge of man Dragon's head is turned to see
the onrush of infinity while Tarr is up, her aim is higher
to blind the moon and fell the scourge of man.

Dragon's head is turned to see the onrush of infinity
he can but laugh and let out flame
which was just how he lost the game.
Dragon's one and only action doomed him them and freed
the town
to live in peace and prosperity, in amongst the families.

But poor Jell's feather were all gone up in smoke
his charred remains were caught inside the mighty giant's throat
which choked.
Tarr flew up and stuck herself into dragon's widening eye
to spite her health and make him cry
for the sake of child, her family, who slept in a nest.

Dragon is blinded, dragon is tilted, dragon is choked,
dead dragon landed, with a bat tree in his breast.
Dead, inert, one dead dragon, one dead dragon's tear
that now flows as the River Aire.

The owl's fate is well remembered, their statues rise above the
city centre.
Their only child was housed anew inside the local village zoo.
"A socially deprived childhood," it should be said, "is not well
spelt in owl vocabulary."

Advertisement copy for Community Policing

I've often tried, more than one or two times
to do summat for these folk.
I have often shared and often cared, over many a pint and a
smoke.

From the Cross of the King
to the Birmingham Ring
my intentions I have made quite clear.

Too much applause and much aplomb
and shaking of hands and many a cheer.
Rather than a thousand men that are pressed
give me just one volunteer.

After 30 years public sector advertisement
I can now advise you in poetry
write to me neither in prose or verse
just have a word with your local P.C.

Special thanks to Phil of the South Manchester Division of
the Greater Manchester Police for helping to Fight Crime
and Protecting People.

On Thin Ice

Bubbles rose through the yellow liquid, ascending before her eyes. Gloria didn't really have the will to pick up the small tankard. She simply sat with her hands on the table, her head resting upon them, watching the bubbles race one another to the surface. Cigarette fumes brushed past her nostrils, shrouding the inn with a cloudy haze. She coughed slightly, unable to prevent herself from following with a frustrated groan.

"You'd be'er drink that mead before it gets warm, Mrs Evestein."

The portly owner, who also doubled as the inn's bartender, must've heard her. Not surprising, since there were no other patrons to make a sound, nor any music playing from a gramophone or wireless.

"*Miss* Evestein," she clarified curtly.

As if it could ever get warm here. The cabby had dropped her off from the station in the morning, and since then the warmest it had been was mildly chilly around midday. Outside, the wind was starting to gust, whistling past the windows and carrying small snowflakes with it. A far cry from the comforting heat of Valharen, a warmth so tangible that just wandering the mountain paths felt like snuggling into a lover's embrace. The job she enjoyed, but the travelling she most definitely did not.

"Ain't you got business to be attendin' to?"

He'd taken the cigarette out of his mouth and put down the glass that he'd been wiping, his hand on his hip, scowling over his double chin, keenly awaiting her departure. Such hospitality. She glanced at her wristwatch. Well, he wasn't wrong.

"Yes, but I shan't be out long."

"What ya talkin' to young Kiarvan 'bout, anyway?"

"That's between him and myself, Mr Felstoff."

With a disappointed grunt, the owner made his way to the back. Gloria decided to give up on her drink before she'd even taken a sip. She just about managed to summon the effort to rise, slinging her handbag over her shoulder and ambling over to the front door of the inn. The encroaching twilight and whistling wind caused her to hesitate, but she didn't have much choice.

The waning sunlight was assisted in illuminating the street by only a couple of lamps, not that there was much to light in the first place. On arrival, Gloria had counted perhaps twenty buildings in total, and most of them were residential. Wrapping her arms around herself and tucking her hands under her armpits (thank goodness she'd at least been sensible enough to bring woollen gloves), she struggled through the gusts across the road. The tips of the distant mountains were distinctly contrasted on the horizon in the orange glow, marking the boundary of the Flats. Vast cloud formations passed silently overhead. How anyone could live up here, surrounded by mile upon mile of seemingly lifeless tundra, was beyond her comprehension.

Reaching the other side, she banged on the door of the first house she came to and waited for Kiarvan to open it, stamping her feet in the cold. Despite his letter being the reason that Gloria had dragged herself to this far and freezing corner of Iskolda, she had yet to meet the man in person.

The door opened and a rather fearsome lady with shoulder-length, straggly, greying hair looked out from a dimly-lit porch. She had tough, pointed features, her bright blue eyes piercing into Gloria's.

"You the Evestein woman?" she asked in a deadpan voice, but before Gloria could bring up her arranged meeting, she continued: "He's not in."

"Oh?" was all Gloria could manage at first, her brow creasing. "W-we agreed we'd meet at this time?"

"I know, but he ain't 'ere. Wen' out, didn't he?"

It didn't make any sense. He'd *asked* her to come here in his letter, said that there were things he couldn't explain in writing and that she needed to see for herself so that she could write up a detailed report for the Arcane Magistrate. Not having enough time to talk with her earlier in the day, he'd told her to drop by around five.

"U-um...well, how long ago? W-where did he go?"

The woman shrugged.

"Dunno, about twenty minutes ago, maybe he felt like goin' for a stroll. He does that."

In this kind of weather? She must be joking, although knowing the people up here, perhaps not.

"Where would he go for a walk?"

"Probably the lake." Her face suddenly took on a more solemn look. "He's always going over to the lake now."

Gloria's confusion only intensified.

"Uh, sorry, what lake?"

The woman produced a slightly dumbfounded expression.

"*The* lake, sweetheart. Lake Ardil. I thought that's why you was 'ere."

She had to think for a moment to make sure her memory wasn't letting her down, but Kiarvan had definitely not mentioned anything in the letter about any lake.

"No, I...well, I don't know exactly why I'm here, honestly. Mr Rhyms was going to tell me what was going on."

"Well, be'er find 'im then, 'eh? You see 'im, you bring 'im back before it gets too late, alrigh'?" She didn't seem that cross, just weary.

"Yes, of course," Gloria agreed.

The door closed.

Well, that was... enlightening. What lake was she on about? And what was Gloria going to do now? She stomped furiously on the slightly muddy ground, trying desperately to warm up her feet even a little, she'd need all of her energy just to go wandering around, searching for... and then she spotted them. Footprints, difficult to make out in the darkness. They weren't hers, they were made with boots, quite freshly imprinted into the shallow mud, pointing away from the house door. Her eyes followed them into the glow of the nearest streetlamp. They headed diagonally across the road in the direction of the mountains.

Nestling her chin into her jacket collar, Gloria began to walk alongside them. How far had he gone? He'd mentioned in the letter that he was a fisherman, but there's nothing he could be doing out there at this time on the lake, and if it *had* been important, surely he'd have said something to this woman, presumably his mother. Passing the small shop on the corner, which looked as though it hadn't stocked fresh goods inside of the last decade, the footprints continued past the remaining houses.

Beyond the corner of the last building, Gloria was greeted by the sight of the vast expanse that surrounded the village. Patches of vegetation dotted the otherwise desolate landscape. There were few forests or even trees to be seen for miles, the ground to the mountains almost as flat as a pancake save for shallow dips and rises.

She didn't notice the lake at first, but as she took in the view, the light bouncing off its icy surface caught her attention. Rather unsurprisingly, it was frozen over, and the footprints were indeed heading in that direction. Ugh, her shoes were a mess, covered around the sides and toes with mud. Embracing her coat tighter than ever, she started striding towards it, unsure of what significance it could hold. Closing in, she saw a shape that didn't belong. There was somebody out there. Somebody who was lying on top.

Gloria reached the edge. Rather tentatively, she took a step onto the ice, testing its strength. It seemed pretty safe. She kept going, glancing down and then up, walking towards the body, her pace speeding up as she gained confidence. Who else could it be but Kiarvan? He wasn't making any movements. She looked down again. Although the twilight was bright enough to shimmer off the ice, she couldn't see her reflection in it... or, thinking about it, *any* reflection, not even the clouded sky.

He wasn't even ten steps away now, face down, his legs sprawled open. She slowed down, moving cautiously. Was he... was he alive? Was he hurt? His thick winter jacket and trousers rustled in the gusts. Gloria walked carefully around him. His arms were forward, his gloved hands up by his head, the jacket's hood covering it. She bent down. He was still as a rock. Her foot inched towards his arm.

"K-Kiarvan?" she uttered, but she could barely hear herself above the wind.

Her shoe knocked against his elbow.

"ARGH!"

She slipped, and before she knew it she was falling, throwing her hands behind her to break the drop. There was a hard but muffled THUMP! as her back contacted the thick ice, pain shooting up from her coccyx and shoulder blades. Taking a few breaths, she pushed her torso up so she could see in front of herself.

The man was on his side, glaring at her. He was breathing heavily, his breath condensing in the cold air. A dense, dark brown beard shrouded a lot of his pale face, but his wide, thickset nose stood out.

"Bloody hell, woman, you scared me!" he yelled in a somewhat high-pitched voice that was in stark contrast to his physique.

The pain was still throbbing through her back, but it was bearable. He picked himself up and then offered her his hand.

"You must be Miss Evestein. I'm Kiarvan. Kiarvan Rhyms. I asked you to come."

He hauled her to her feet and brushed off her coat.

"You all right? Sorry if I—"

"Yes, yes, nothing broken, I think," Gloria replied, making light of it. As she looked around, the aching began to move to the back of her mind. "What, uh, what're you doing out here? We were supposed to meet, Mr Rhyms."

Kiarvan looked down at the ice where he'd been lying.

"Yeah, sorry, I just... I forgot the time, just wanted to come out here for a bit before I brought you over. Call me Kiarvan, by the way."

"Okay, Kiarvan. Brought me over to see what?"

He turned back to her, their eyes meeting. He had a gaze like his mother's that Gloria felt could see almost completely through her, but his irises were a strong green.

"This."

Kiarvan motioned downwards with both hands. Despite the woman's voiced expectations of why she'd come here, Gloria was still somewhat taken aback.

"The lake?"

"Yes."

"But... but why? What's going on?"

"See for yourself."

With him looking on expectantly, Gloria turned her eyes downward... but there was nothing there. The fading sun lit up the lake, but below the thick sheet of ice, only a dark abyss greeted her.

"What d'you mean? I don't see anything."

He wrinkled his brow.

"Hmm... come this way, then, over there. Maybe you'll see it there."

She tried to keep up with his stiff pace, their feet stomping across the surface. Kiarvan was constantly looking down, searching for something. He didn't seem remotely worried about their safety.

"Sh-shouldn't we be more careful?" she called out after him. "Isn't there a chance we could fall through some thin ice?"

"Not a chance, lass. Ice is so thick, you could jump up and down on it and nothin' would happen. That's the problem."

Once again, Gloria wasn't feeling any more clued in.

"W-what? Please, just tell me what's going on!"

He stopped abruptly, spinning around. Her eyes pleaded with him to explain.

"I... there... this isn't..." Taking a moment or so to breathe, he tried again, speaking up so she could hear him. "This lake, something's wrong with it. I... three months ago, my fiancée, she... she..." Going on was difficult. Tears were beginning to form around his eyes. "...She drowned, here, in the lake. We were out on the boat, she fell..." He was just about able to fight back the urge to break down. "She went under. I tried, I *tried*, I did everythin', but in this water you can't survive long. She was scared, she panicked, the cold stopped her from..."

"It's okay." Despite the cold, Gloria took her hands out from her armpits and gripped his shoulders, trying to console him. He whimpered slightly before going on.

"If anythin' ends up in the lake, it's usually gone forever. We can't go into the water, you need specialists from the city to bring their divin' equipment. My Rachel, I needed to get her back, even if only to bury her. I asked the divers to come as soon as they could... but then, a few days later, before they could get here, the lake froze over. It froze in the middle of autumn! And it's still like this. That's not natural."

She was trying to take in what he was saying, wondering if grief was clouding his sense of judgement, but then again, as a fisherman who had probably grown up here, Kiarvan likely knew what he was taking about. He gently pushed her back and pounded his foot against the glassy surface.

"See? I can stamp on it, smash it with tools. Nothing happens. The ice is so thick, always has been since the day it froze. It's not right! I haven't been able to fish in months. We're used to ice fishing in the winter, but we can't cut through this at all!"

"Okay, okay, calm down." Gloria tried to speak as softly as she could over the wind. "So, you brought me here because you think something's wrong? Something unnatural is at work?"

"I don't *think*, lass, I *know*." Kiarvan couldn't have sounded more convinced. "Come, I can show you."

He started off again across the ice, and Gloria was about to follow him to see whatever it was that was bothering him... when she stopped. Something, something was stopping her. What was it? Through the gusting wind, she had to strain her ears to make out another noise. *Was* it another sound? It was so faint that perhaps she was just imagining it. A sort of... muffled thumping? She looked around. Besides Kiarvan, the only thing around her was the expanse of countryside, quite beautifully lit by the slowly darkening sky. Confused, she glanced down.

And leapt into the air, releasing a loud shriek.

A woman was looking up at her, blue eyes wide, brunette hair waving around her, her whole body visible in the dark water underneath Gloria's shoes, touching the ice with one hand and banging her other fist against it, her mouth open in a silent cry and blasting out bubbles, moving in a fashion that suggested speech. Gloria must be seeing things. She closed her eyes and opened them again. The woman was still there, pounding against the frozen surface, her soaked woollen clothing not seeming to prove an impediment to her will to free herself. She kept screaming, but Gloria couldn't hear it; she could only watch her blued lips open and close.

HELP ME.

"What is it?"

Kiarvan had hurried back over and was looking down beside her. Gloria frantically turned her head to him.

"D-d-you see her?"

He didn't seem phased, as if he couldn't see anything and was just staring into the water, and yet his answer betrayed that notion.

"Yes."

She looked back down.

"W-we, we need to do something!"

"No need," he said regretfully. "She's dead."

Gloria snapped her eyes to him, shocked.

"WHAT?! Look at her, she needs help, man!"

"No, you don't understand, Miss Evestein." He locked his eyes into hers once more. "That's Maria. She died not long after my Rachel. Drowned. I've seen her almost every day since."

What? How? Gloria couldn't help but return her eyes to the desperate woman, pounding all it was worth, desperate for the surface, for air... and yet, she never seemed to run out of breath. It was erupting from her open mouth, the bubbles bursting relentlessly against the ice. Gloria didn't know what to think. Fear and sadness were competing to dominate her emotions. Was she —

The woman suddenly jerked, yanked downwards by something, and with her arms reaching skyward and what seemed to be a final cry, she disappeared straight down into the abyss. Gone. Gloria instinctively dropped to her knees, her gloves scratching at the ice.

"Huh? What... where'd she go?"

"Back." His words were grave. "They always go back eventually."

Getting to her feet, Gloria raised her hands in front of her face in exasperation.

"'Back! Back *where*!"

"I dunno, do I? That's why I asked you to come here!" he shouted back. "So, you could see it, explain it, tell us and the magistrate what's going on!"

"I don't know the theory, Mr Rhyms." She reverted back to his surname unintentionally, probably trying to hammer the reality of the situation into him. "I-I'm not an expert on the phenomena, I just report it to those who do so they can come to conclusions, make decisions."

His expression flicked between confusion and frustration. "So, I have to wait for the official report to know what's going on here! You can't give us *any* answers?"

Gloria looked back down to where the woman had been. What in Hell was happening? She'd seen a few things in the course of her admittedly short career, but nothing like this. She wasn't lying, she hadn't studied the theory, but she *had* read the reports that she'd helped get written, she'd reviewed plenty of cases of magical and other anomalies. After all, that's how she'd become interested in this line of work. Wracking her brains, she tried to think if there was anything she'd come across that was similar to this.

"The ice is unnatural, right? Been here for three months, and it's always been this thick?"

"Yes, yes."

She knew that it would be freezing, but nevertheless she couldn't help but slump down onto the ice. Kiarvan followed suit next to her.

"She drowned, yes? Maria, was it? After Rachel and before the lake froze over?"

"Y-yes..."

"How? How could she drown right after? Surely people around here are careful when going out on the lake?"

"We think, um..." He didn't want to say it. "...We think she drowned herself. Her and Rachel, they were... very close. She was always upset after my Rachel died, almost as broken as me." Swallowing hard, he sniffed again. "She, she told me she couldn't take it, couldn't take losing her best friend. You've seen what it's like here. Not many of us livin' in Ardil, it's a small community. You lose one person, it's hard, but to lose one of the people you're closest with? And now for us to lose two of them in a couple of months?"

Unsure of what to say, Gloria sat quietly, feeling the wind across her face. She almost couldn't feel the cold any more.

"Anyone see her do it?"

"No. She disappeared one night. The next time anyone saw her, it was me, and I saw her just like you did."

Could they be sure it was suicide?

"It seems to me, Kiarvan, that something in this lake is taking people, holding onto them. The icing, my guess is that it was formed to..." She had to find the words, feeling strange for saying them aloud: "...to trap the souls of the dead."

Her words sank in after a few seconds. He sat there, slumped on the ice next to her, looking helpless.

"So, um... w-who, w-what is doing it?"

"No idea." She desperately wish she knew. "Anything strange happened in this lake over the years? Any ships sink, many other people drowned in it?"

He mulled over her question.

"A few fishing boats have gone down in the past, and some deaths on the lake, but not that many. No more than you'd expect."

No immediate red flags there, then. Damn, she really couldn't help him. It would be up to the magistrate to decide what was going on and what could be done.

"Well, Kiarvan, there's not much else we can do here." She thought of something. "What were you doing when I got here? Were you..." Then it came to her. "...Were you looking for Rachel?"

He lowered his eyes.

"Yes. Sometimes I see her under the ice. She's not like Maria, she isn't screaming, trying to get out. She, uh... she seems to... accept it? I think she knows she's dead, but she isn't trying to escape. She always looks so peaceful, a bit sad, but peaceful. She... she smiles at..."

All this time he'd been successful in holding back his emotions, but now they finally got the better of him, and he started to sob, muffling it as best he could. Gloria shuffled over and put her arms around him.

"It's okay. She misses you, and you miss her, I know." She let go and looked him dead in the eye. "But you can't keep coming here. She's gone. You have to let her go."

Through coughs and sniffles, he returned her gaze, his eyes squinting through tears.

"I can't. She's all I have besides Mum, and she's down there." He slapped the frozen surface in futility. "She's trapped! *Trapped*! You said it yourself! I have to keep comin' so that she can see my face, have something to comfort her, someone to talk to, even though we can't hear each other..."

"Kiarvan, she's dead. You're not speaking to her, you're speaking to a memory, an image. You can't keep doing this."

Gloria wasn't actually sure about that—not really knowing what's going on, how could she be?—but she felt that it was in his interests not to torture himself, to linger on the dead. Perhaps, if what he was talking to *was* indeed more than simply a memory, seeing her lover every day might not be good for her spirit either, even if it was a temporary comfort. Gloria was worried that the woman who was appearing to him wasn't who he thought she was, but she didn't want to voice those concerns just now.

"H-how do you know?" he choked.

"Trust me. I'm not an expert, but I *do* know about these things. I've seen stuff before."

"Well... okay." He used his hands to help him stand up before pulling her up as well. "Maybe... maybe I will see her less."

Well, that was something.

"That's all I'd ask for now. Come on, we should be going. I need to call back to Karinth, let the magistrate know what we've found. Do you have a working phone?"

"Yeah we do, you can use it, no problem."

They began to trudge back across the frozen lake, Gloria out in front. She was quite curious to question him further about his fiancée, but she didn't dare say anything, not wishing to stir up more painful memories. She held her coat tightly shut against the wind. Her questions were replaced by the sight of that woman, slamming her fist against the lid of her watery tomb. Her heart skipped beats. She closed her eyes, trying desperately to dispel the memory, to force another, happier one into its place, but the darkness simply made it more vivid, sharpening the look of utter despair on her face as she screamed. It was utterly terrifying, and in the back of her mind—behind this grotesque memory—she knew that it was going to be some time before she could properly sleep again, if ever.

Her eyes reopened... and Gloria lurched to a halt, almost tumbling over, looking down at the glassy ice. There was someone looking up at her, but it wasn't the woman who was plaguing her mind.

It took her longer than it should have to realise who the figure was. It was *her*. The same long brown summer coat, the same darkened skin, the same intensely brown hair tied up in two buns. And yet, it *wasn't* her. Her reflection looked... neater? Her real hair was becoming a bit of a mess now, being battered by the elements, and yet the hair buns of the woman who stared back at her were tidily-kept, as if she'd only just done them. Was she in fact looking better than she thought she was? That notion was quickly dispelled as some of her loose hairs flapped across her face, in stark contrast to her reflection who showed nothing of the sort.

"What is it?" came Kiarvan's voice from behind as he caught up to her.

Gloria almost didn't hear him, his words being more of an echo in the background. She stood transfixed, not taking her eyes off of her reflection... but it wasn't her reflection. It was an imposter. She should be terrified, said the little voice in her mind, she should be running, running as fast as she could, as far away from this place as her legs could carry her. Still, she stood there, unable to move, unable to say anything. She should be horrified, but instead she felt a strange and comforting warmth inside. The alternate her stared back, the face not displaying any discernible emotion, but the eyes seemed to convey kindness and friendly reassurance. Gradually, the dark lips curved into a genuine smile, and despite the fear she knew should be welling inside of her, Gloria couldn't help but smile back.

CRACK!

The reflection was instantly shattered as the ice gave way beneath her feet. She began to descend, the lake and mountains whooshing upwards, feeling the sudden sensation of her stomach flying skyward and the water's freezing grip rapidly spreading up her leg to her waist and then her torso as she fell.

With her heart practically exploding from her chest and but a moment for her mind to comprehend what was about to happen, Gloria was only able to emit a final scream of pure, unadulterated terror before the world above vanished from view and she was fully immersed in the dark embrace of the icy waters below.

A Collection of Poetry

A Broken Spirit

They answered the call
and marched to war
with pride and promise
to stand as heroes
Against all.

He returned alone
with pain in his heart
more painful
than to loose
where once there was a leg
an arm
a face
that once won him a bride
and now he just wants to hide.

She is gone
as he knew she would
she had tried
but it was no good
to start each day
he knew she had
to look away.

So now he sits alone
and wonders why
as Iraq comes flooding in
where his comrades lie
and now his wish
is just to die.

Yet he knows
he has to live
to face adversity
and over come
just to survive
it's man's instinct
to stay alive.

In My Mind

Did you wonder when you passed this way
would you pass this way again?
Did you wonder if those two lions
looking so benign gave any hint
of what was to happen when
you were in the line?

Did you think on the whistles shrill command
go forward to be shot or if not
stand to be shot by comrades
on demand of those in bunkers far behind.

We'll never know how your body fell
or where you now lie
but we will lay a poppy here
by the Mennen Gate
shed a tear for your memory
and go upon our way
to wonder why our young are still
sacrificed today.

Maybe a wife and children
or parents left to cry
never to know how you died
or where you now lie
but Poppies mark this
unknown spot
as we make our sad goodbye.

EXPLOSION

Red speckled rain,
limbs broken bodies.
The Jihad hatred
causes so much pain.

Darkness falls,
rescuers frost bitten breath
cast staccato dancing shadows
in the floodlit air.
Hope dims as relatives,
stand and stare.

A voice in perfect pitch
abide with me,
for the souls now gone
bodies no more to be.

Grief and anger burns.
Vengeance is required again
and so the cycle turns
with malevolent hate inspired,
and relatives cry in vain.

An Ode to You

How should I praise you
as the beauty of the Rose in bloom
as bright as the Lilly in the valley
or as sweet as the song of the Lark
in the clear morning air
soaring above the world
without a single care.

How should I praise you
with a word from the Bard
as like a summer day
or as fresh morning dew
opening the flowers in May.

Or the warmth of Winters glow
as round the fire we stay
with snowflakes all around
and children out to play
until the sun goes down.

These are things of beauty
as on our way we go
these words I send to you
I will always love you so.

Poème

L'éternité nous rejoindra-t-elle jamais ?
Je ne connais pas sa couleur ni son odeur,
Mais sa présence me manque.
Je me retourne,
Mon visage n'est plus le mien,
Je n'aperçois que mon ombre.
Alors je lève mes yeux vers ce ciel solitaire,
Je voudrais voir les étoiles afin de peindre leur visage.

Histoires courtes

Le mari

Roger et sa femme Adélie s'étaient mariés il y a un an dans la Basilique Notre-Dame, dans la ville de Nice. Le 15 août 2005, les cloches de l'église, pour un instant semblaient ne sonner que pour eux, trois enfants habillés de blanc, Sophie, Éléonore et le petit Carl, tous des enfants d'amie de la ville, de Madame Renée, amie d'enfance d'Adélie qui les suivaient dans l'allée centrale de l'église. Le soleil ruisselait sur les arbres et sur l'avenue Jean Médecin. À la sortie, une colombe blanche de la paix s'envola et ils jetèrent le bouquet à la foule. Marie-Armande, une demoiselle venue de Paris le rattrapa, ce serait-elle la future mariée ? Beaucoup s'étaient déplacés de loin pour l'événement car ils appréciaient la compagnie d'Adélie et de Roger et voulaient célébrer ce moment avec eux.

Roger pratiquait le sport, le basket pour entretenir sa santé. Il était membre du club de sport et faisait également de la natation. Ils avaient acheté un trois pièces, après avoir visité de nombreux appartements dans les hauteurs de Cimiez pour que leur fille ou leur fils puisse avoir sa propre chambre.

Roger disait qu'il aimerait sa fille ou son fils autant que sa femme. En secret, il espérait un fils pour pouvoir l'emmener au sport. Adélie espérait une petite fille, pour pouvoir partager sa féminité, et la voir essayer son maquillage.

Madame Renée prit le bus et discuta dans le salon avec Adélie, elle lui dit à quel point sa joie était grande de savoir qu'elle était enceinte d'un mois.

— Nos enfants, même s'ils n'ont pas le même âge pourraient se rencontrer et mes filles seront comme des grandes sœurs, et mon fils Carl comme un grand frère, ajouta Madame Renée. Madame Renée et Adélie discutaient encore des écoles de Nice et de la première communion de Sophie et des préparatifs qui seraient nécessaires pour le baptême du petit d'Adélie. Adélie pensa qu'elle choisirait Madame Renée comme marraine mais qu'elle lui en parlerait plus tard.

Jason, un ami de l'université de droit l'appela pour savoir s'il pouvait passer dans la soirée pour discuter.

— Je te prie de bien vouloir m'excuser, j'étais à New York et je n'ai pas pu assister au mariage, mais j'aimerais vous faire un cadeau, dit Jason.

En apprenant que la femme de Roger, Adélie, était enceinte d'un mois, il dit :

— Je vous offre une séance photo souvenir à vous trois et à votre futur bébé, chez une amie photographe, Mathilde, qui habite à Nice, et encore toutes mes félicitations à toi et à ta belle épouse, dit Jason à Roger.

— Merci infiniment Jason, répondit Roger et il ajouta :

— La photo sert à capturer la vie, et rien n'est plus précieux pour moi que ma femme et mon futur enfant, je te remercie du fond du cœur, répondit Roger, et si tu viens à Nice nous irons dîner Italien, des pizzas, comme tu les aimes.

Ainsi allait la vie, de la naissance à la mort et il pensait que c'était le début d'une grande aventure et Roger regarda la photo du mariage avec Adélie il y a seulement trois mois. La vue de la photo lui rappelait les sons des cloches de l'église, c'était pour lui le début de sa vie d'adulte, après tout, n'avaient-ils pas fêter l'enterrement de sa vie de garçon comme celui de la vie de jeune fille d'Adélie il n'y a pas si longtemps.

Mais Adélie se dit qu'il se préoccupait beaucoup du sport, et restait malgré tout amateur, mais elle était follement amoureuse et se dit que cela viendrait.

— Je vais courir tous les matins pour garder la forme pour notre match de basket en amateur, je nage deux fois par semaine et je vais au stade jouer trois fois par semaine avec mes coéquipiers ; nous allons partir à Lyon et nous espérons gagner le match, dit Roger.

Quand son ami Jason vient dîner, Roger proposa à son ami de venir avec lui pour voir le match, mais Jason devait plaider à la cour.

— Demande à Adélie, ta femme, de filmer et si vous gagnez, nous visionnerons le film tous les trois, répondit Jason.

Roger avait passé l'examen médical et le docteur de famille disait qu'il était en bonne santé. Roger était heureux et pensait que la vie lui souriait. Il traversa Nice à pied sans trop d'effort par cette chaleur propre à la Côte d'Azur.

N'avait-il pas la plus belle femme, la plus gentille, la plus attentionnée ? Une semaine avant le match, il vit du sang dans ses urines mais refusa d'appeler le médecin de peur de ne pas pouvoir participer au match amateur Nice-Lyon. Le sang ne cessa qu'après un quart d'heure.

Mais il ne dit rien à personne, même s'il se sentait soudainement ivre de fatigue rien qu'en allant dans sa chambre. Et ivre de fatigue tout le long de la journée.

Adélie et Roger prirent le train pour Lyon. Ils s'installèrent dans le train et Roger ouvrit un livre à une page au hasard se sentant trop fatigué pour lire, un livre qu'il avait jeté dans son sac : « Je voudrais mourir au plus intense de la vie pour ne pas voir venir la mort, en plein feu de l'action. »

Il eut soudainement la nausée mais n'en parla pas à Adélie. Il avait des douleurs, sentant le besoin d'uriner, se leva fréquemment pour utiliser les toilettes du train, Adélie s'inquiéta, mais elle était préoccupée par ce petit bébé qui bougeait en elle. Son ventre avait déjà un peu de volume grâce à son quatrième mois de grossesse.

— Tiens Roger, pose ta main sur mon ventre, tu sentiras le petit, dit Adélie.

Et il avait senti la vie. Il ne désirait rien d'autre que de voir naitre son petit, pour le voir grandir, de petit garçon à un jour homme. Ainsi va la vie, pensait-il, et je serai bientôt père, puis grand-père. J'enseignerai à mon enfant une saine crainte et amour de Dieu.

Le lendemain, c'était le match. Roger se sentait ivre de fatigue après une perte de sang encore plus accentuée qu'avant.

Son coéquipier, Marc, lui envoya le ballon, il était proche du panier, la foule criait, Adélie filmait.

Dans un effort suprême, Roger courait en tapant le ballon contre le sol, puis sauta, marqua un point pour son équipe mais s'effondra sur le sol.

Les secours arrivèrent, il y avait du sang sur son short. Mais il était déjà mort. Le cancer de la prostate et son dernier effort avait eu raison de la vie. Adélie ne voulait plus jamais rien filmer et pleura tous les jours jusqu'à la naissance de l'enfant.

Le médecin la contacta, et dit :

— Mais pourquoi ne m'en a-t-il pas parlé, on aurait peut-être pu le soigner. Il devait y avoir du sang dans ses urines pendant longtemps.

Il était parti dans le feu de l'action et son enterrement eut lieu trois jours après, dans l'église Notre-Dame de Nice. Le soleil ruisselait sur les arbres et l'avenue Jean-Médecin, les oiseaux chantaient, les cloches retentirent, mais Adélie pleurait, Madame Renée et beaucoup d'invités du mariage étaient réunis, car c'était un homme aimé de tous, non il n'aurait pas dû quitter ce monde, pensa-t-on et il fut regretté de sa famille et de ses proches aussi longtemps qu'ils vécurent.

Le pêcheur

La journée fut longue pour le pêcheur, il allait sur sa barque par la rivière. Déjà le soleil avait laissé une lumière pourpre, de mauve et d'or glissant sur les eaux. De sa barque, il observait. Il espérait rejoindre le petit port avant l'apparition de la première étoile. Il fixa les yeux sur le port, qu'il distingua à peine tellement il était loin. Puis il contempla les poissons et les compta, il avait dix-huit sardines. Et oui, il devait trouver quelqu'un pour les lui racheter avant le départ du camion pour le marché. Il espérait six ou sept pièces d'or, bien qu'il aurait souhaité garder quatre ou cinq sardines pour rendre plus consistant son maigre dîner. Aujourd'hui et encore demain, il fut contraint de vendre la totalité de sa pêche.

Il savait bien qu'avec sa canne à pêche de fortune, il n'atteindrait jamais les cinq cents grammes de poisson. Toujours, il resterait condamné à la misère. Sa canne à pêche était du modèle le plus simple et lui avait déjà coûté douze pièces d'or.

Réinvestir dans une deuxième, pour le soir venu ramener le double était impossible. Il devait se contenter de quelques pièces d'or, six ou sept, ce qui ne lui donnerait jamais de la viande.

Mais à nouveau, tout en rejoignant le port et en attachant le bateau, il compta les étoiles. C'était avec quelques autres camarades, ses amies.

« Mon Dieu que la lune est belle, » pensa-t-il. Personne ne lui avait dit qu'elle avait plusieurs visages, variant selon l'heure, la position de la terre, son mouvement et les saisons.

Et oui, il l'aimait, la nature, la liberté, la lune et le ciel étoilé. Il y avait encore quelques gouttes d'eau sur ses mains. Ses mains étaient gercées, mais il aimait la vie.

Au loin, toute la journée l'usine avait craché de la fumée. Du travail à l'usine, voilà ce dont il avait rêvé l'année dernière, mais pour acheter le journal et mettre de côté de quoi téléphoner, il avait déjà essayé de se passer de pain pendant trois jours.

Et, le jour de l'entretien à l'usine, il s'était présenté le ventre creux. En effet, la plus grande partie de son alimentation était constituée de pain. Mais après avoir obtenu un entretien, un homme à la barbe rasé lui avait juste dit :

— Candidat suivant !

Le poste d'ouvrier à l'usine refusé, il ne lui restait que la pêche et son unique joie fut de voir le soleil sans nuage. Jamais plus, il ne ferait l'impasse sur une journée de pêche. « L'usine pouvait cracher de la fumée, je m'en fous, je contemplerai les poissons. »

« Pourvu que ma canne à pêche ne lâche pas », pensa-t-il. La misère était déjà grande et ce loyer de cent cinquante pièces d'or, si seulement il pouvait vivre sur le bateau, mais c'était une barque. Non, il voulait les vomir plutôt que de devoir payer encore.

Rien n'annulait la pêche, ni le froid, ni le vent, ni la maladie, ni ses mains gercées.

Du moment que sa canne à pêche ne lâche pas, son humble prière était :

« Mon Dieu, mon Dieu, préservez ma canne à pêche. »

Tous les soirs, il l'essuyait avec le même chiffon et ses chaussettes avaient de larges trous. Les semelles de ses chaussures étaient décollées, mais il ne pensa guère à en acheter de nouvelles. Avec la colle d'un ami, cinq fois déjà André avait recollé les semelles.

Non, non, il n'y pensait même plus, il regardait attentivement où il mettait les pieds, eh oui, il fallait bien éviter les flaques d'eau pour que ses bottines tiennent la route.

« Mon Dieu, mon Dieu, faites que ma canne à pêche ne lâche pas, » murmura-t-il à nouveau. Sans ça, la rue.

« Mon Dieu, mon Dieu, faites que ma canne à pêche tienne, » dit-il encore.

Bien sur la solidité de sa barque laissait à désirer, mais chaque matin, il embarquait à nouveau.

Mais pas question de rejoindre la mer avec une barque si fragile. La mer, la mer, il en rêvait. C'était là où il y avait le plus de poissons. Des maquereaux, des langoustes, des soles, des espadons...

Il y en avait en mer, du poisson. Mais sa barque fragile ne résistait qu'à l'eau des rivières. André avait laissé tomber depuis trente-cinq ans maintenant l'idée de devenir pêcheur d'eau salée à la place d'eau douce, pêcheur de mer.

Et pourtant, elle n'était pas loin, la mer. Il avait essayé d'économiser pour acheter le dit bateau.

Cela fut également impossible, pour économiser une pièce d'argent, il fallait déjà ne pas manger de pain pendant cinq jours et le bateau de mer coûtait cinq cents pièces d'or.

Parce qu'il était en retard sur son loyer, tous les jours, passé la trêve hivernale, le propriétaire le menaçait d'expulsion. Et, quand il ne le menaçait pas, il en faisait des cauchemars. Il voulait toujours savoir s'il aurait les cent cinquante pièces d'or pour le loyer. Un jour par mois, il ne lui était pas possible de dormir un peu plus et s'il le faisait, il louperait alors le vendeur du marché qui partait avec le camion de cinq heures trente vers la ville de Paris. S'il dormait, ne serait-ce qu'un jour par semaine, il manquerait alors cinq pièces d'or pour le loyer.

Paris, oui, il en avait entendu parler, mais jamais André n'avait pu s'y rendre.

Le vol du petit cheval blanc

Voici, à l'écurie du Mirage Eternel que se présente Thomas.

— Bonjour M. John, je me présente, l'inspecteur Thomas, je suis venu relever les indices concernant le vol de Mozart, le petit cheval blanc.

— Mozart a disparu hier soir, ou bien dans la nuit, dit M. John.

— Vous aviez les caméras de vidéosurveillance ? demanda Thomas.

— Oui, tout à fait, souhaitez-vous les examiner ? demanda M. John.

— Oui, bien sûr, M. John.

— Suivez-moi.

Ils entrèrent dans la salle de vidéo surveillance, Thomas et M. John visionnèrent les cassettes de vidéo surveillance.

Au début, la nuit à l'écurie du Mirage semblait se dérouler paisiblement. Mais voilà que vers trois heures du matin, toutes les caméras se sont simultanément dirigées vers le ciel étoilé, seule la caméra de l'extérieur fonctionnait. De là, toutes reflétaient la grande ourse, puis la petite ourse et enfin jusqu'au matin, fixèrent la lune prise et reprise sous plusieurs angles.

Le ciel étoilé était semblable à l'humanité, des millions et des milliards d'âmes qui vécurent ici et nous éclairaient là-bas, de passage, les milliards d'âmes ou bien des étoiles vivent à des années lumières, emportées par le vent, le songe, les tourments, tel le firmament.

Mais seules les plus pures, les plus belles resplendissaient là-haut, avait expliqué la fille de M. John, Sophie.

La constellation était la résonnance divine des plus belles âmes de l'humanité, disait-elle. Celles du temps d'avant, du temps de toujours.

Les étoiles étaient la frêle résonnance de l'humanité qui tendait vers l'absolu, expliqua Sophie. Oui, l'éternel était leur demeure.

— Je ne comprends pas, comment toutes les caméras ont été court-circuitées, et chose étrange, il n'y avait pas le son de l'écurie, seul la musique de la « Flûte Enchantée » de Mozart jouait, dit Thomas.

— Nous avons à faire à un habile technicien, dit M. John.

— Il nous joue un tour, répondit Thomas.

— Il me semble que oui, répliqua M. John.

— Avez-vous mis le cheval en vente ? demanda Thomas.

— Oui tout à fait.

— Qui est venu le voir ?

— Trois personnes sont venues le voir ici, à l'écurie du Mirage Eternel, dit M. John.

— Les trois voulaient l'acquérir, toutes à un très bon prix, toutes se le disputaient, ajouta M. John. Mozart a été entraîné ici, ma fille Sophie, s'occupe de lui depuis sa naissance. Depuis que je l'ai mis en vente, elle pleure, et ne parle plus et refuse de manger.

— J'espère que ça va s'arranger, répondit l'inspecteur Thomas, puis il ajouta :

— Y-a-t-il des traces de pneus à l'extérieur ? Et il me faudrait le nom des trois acheteurs.

— Je n'ai que le nom qu'ils ont bien voulu me donner, tous montaient très bien à cheval.

— Merci de bien vouloir bloquer l'accès de l'écurie à tout camion ou voiture et je vous prie d'aller au village à cheval ou à vélo, dit l'inspecteur Thomas. Pendant ce temps, je vais examiner les traces de pneus, ajouta l'inspecteur Thomas.

Alors se mit à jouer à nouveau « La Flûte Enchantée » de Mozart.

Thomas parut surpris et dit :

— Voilà que le voleur nous observe et semble avoir de l'avance sur l'enquête, ça a l'air d'être quelqu'un de malin. C'est loin d'être une affaire simple. Peut-être que les trois noms des acheteurs ne nous mèneront nulle part. Mozart s'est-il fait remarqué récemment en compétition de saut d'obstacle ?

— Oui tout à fait, lors des dernières qualifications aux championnats de France de saut d'obstacle des chevaux de cinq ans, dit M. John et il ajouta :

— Tenez, voilà un article paru dans « L'éperon, » ma fille Sophie est la cavalière, le journaliste en parle comme si c'était un nouvel espoir pour les Jeux Olympiques, le journaliste parle de Mozart comme si c'était le nouveau Milton. Malgré cela, à cause de son jeune âge, je n'ai pas pu obtenir assez d'argent des sponsors. Et ma fille Sophie s'étant laissée emporter par l'espoir de la victoire de cette compétition, lors du barrage au chrono, a pris beaucoup de risques. Mozart a rattrapé ses erreurs en survolant les obstacles qu'ils ont franchis à pleine vitesse. Les sponsors ont dit qu'à cette vitesse-là, elle le mènerait à la faute lors des épreuves de six ans. Ils ont néanmoins gagné l'épreuve.

— Je vois que Mozart pouvait intéresser de nombreux cavaliers, mais il est exclu de faire d'un cheval volé un cheval de concours, poursuivit Thomas.

Il ajouta :

— Je vais récupérer les noms des cavaliers Français auprès de la Fédération Française d'équitation et également étrangers habitant en France ainsi que les noms de propriétaires de fermes, de haras et de centre équestre. Je vais également demander à la police des frontières de bloquer tout passage d'un petit cheval blanc. Je vous tiendrai au courant de l'avancée de mes recherches.

Ils entendirent « Requiem de Mozart » jouer depuis la chambre de Sophie et M. John s'inquiéta beaucoup pour sa fille. Vient l'heure du déjeuner :

— Je ne veux rien manger, je n'ai pas faim, tant que je ne revois pas Mozart, ce petit cheval blanc que j'aime tant. Il était un prodige, un surdoué du saut d'obstacle, un virtuose, jamais aucun autre cheval ne pourra le remplacer. Je ne peux pas vivre sans lui. Il ne me reste qu'à disparaitre, rien ni personne ne pourra jamais me consoler. Ce cheval était un virtuose qui comprenait instinctivement ma volonté de cavalière. Son galop et chaque saut étaient semblables à une envolée lyrique, je ne vis que pour l'embrasser et le revoir, comprends papa que sans lui je me laisse mourir.

— Mais ma petite, ici à l'écurie du Mirage il y aura bientôt des naissances de nombreux poulains et je t'en offrirai un, si seulement tu voulais l'oublier et t'attacher à un autre.

Sophie mangea une bouchée de pain et remonta dans sa chambre écouter « Requiem de Mozart ». M. John téléphona immédiatement à Thomas :

— Ma fille se laisse mourir sans Mozart, je suis très inquiet, avez-vous du nouveau ?

— J'ai récupéré des traces de pneus d'un camion Mercedes différent du camion et de la voiture que vous possédez, je peux vous assurer que l'enquête avancera bientôt, répliqua Thomas.

— Très bien, faites vite, ma fille s'affaiblie.

Pour Sophie toutes les merveilles du monde semblaient être contenues dans un seul pas de Mozart, grâce à sa beauté et à sa grâce, toute la beauté du monde semblait émaner de chacun de ses mouvements et toute l'élégance et la puissance du monde jaillissaient de chacun de ses sauts.

Jamais l'écurie du Mirage n'avait eu un si bon cheval et maintenant qu'allaient-ils devenir ?

Mozart, le cheval blanc était semblable à un rayon de soleil venu du ciel, pour éclairer la terre terne. C'était, et surtout pour Sophie, comme si le soleil de leur vie avait à jamais disparu.

Mozart avait été volé par un ancien cavalier professionnel, peu scrupuleux, trafiquant en tout genre. Il avait embarqué dans son camion Mercedes mais arrivé à l'écurie, Mozart refusa de manger.

Alors, Paul, le voleur décida de le mettre au champ pour lui remonter le moral. Le champ était entouré d'une barrière blanche de deux mètres vingt qu'il pensait qu'un cheval de cinq ans ne pourrait pas franchir.

La nuit tombée, il alla se coucher, Mozart avait brouté de l'herbe et repris des forces et à peine le soleil levé, dès l'aurore, il galopa vers la barrière et franchit les deux mètres vingt avec aisance.

Ayant fréquenté ces chemins lors de promenades avec Sophie, il rejoignit sans peine l'écurie du Mirage. Là, il hennit, réveilla Sophie et M. John.

— Voilà Mozart, dit Sophie. C'est le plus beau jour de ma vie !

— Quel miracle à l'écurie du Mirage ! dit M. John.

Puis il ajouta :

— Je vais prévenir tout de suite l'inspecteur Thomas.

Sophie mit tout de suite le CD de « La flûte enchantée de Mozart. » et elle entama de le brosser avec un bouchon puis une brosse douce.

— Papa, tu ne vas pas le vendre... supplia Sophie.

— Non, ma fille, je vais en vendre trois autres, répondit M. John.

« La Flûte Enchantée » jouait toujours. Thomas arriva et fit venir un technicien pour installer un système d'alarme plus sécurisé. Puis il ajouta :

— Je poursuivrai mes recherches jusqu'à la fin, le voleur doit se trouver dans une écurie des alentours.

Avant l'arrivée du technicien, soudainement ils entendirent « Requiem de Mozart » et à la fin du morceau de musique ils entendirent un coup de feu.

Paul s'était suicidé d'une balle dans la tête.

Nice, le 30 Juillet 2019

Bouffi et Crédulon, après avoir mangé une pizza à midi dans le vieux Nice, allèrent à travers la vieille ville en direction du château. Ils marchèrent au milieu des sillons de la vieille ville et appréciaient les façades colorées de couleur du soleil, ocre rouge et jaune. C'était une belle après-midi d'été. La lumière du soleil ruisselait et leurs ombres dansaient. Ils allaient souvent à l'église et étaient très croyants. Ils goûtèrent aux joies spirituelles tout en profitant de la vie.

— Et si on s'arrêtait pour boire une bière, cours Saleya ? demanda Bouffi.

Crédulon accepta, ils en burent finalement trois. Presque ivres, ils décidèrent de se rendre au château. C'était une course à la vie, une course à la mort. Le soleil, haut dans le ciel, tapait sur la colline du château, en cette après-midi de juillet. Ils pensaient qu'ils n'arriveraient jamais à destination. Il était 15 h 06. Bouffi et Crédulon virent le château et plus tard après avoir monté la dernière partie de la colline, ils arrivèrent au château du vieux Nice.

Bouffi et Crédulon virent soudainement danser les étoiles et le ciel descendre sur eux. Une voix dans les nuées les interpella.

Là, ils virent les silhouettes, de vivants et de morts. Transportés par leur âme, transportés par leur être. Transportés dans l'au-delà qui se reflétait ici-bas. Une vision d'un monde nouveau les stupéfia et pour un instant les rendit muet, tremblant de peur. Mais la terre était ferme sous leurs pas mais ayant beaucoup bu, ils avancèrent doucement.

L'espoir et la terreur furent pour un instant mélangé. Ils levèrent les mains vers le ciel et crièrent de joie et d'effroi. Puis ils se mirent à prier.

— Je vous salue Marie pleine de grâce, dit Bouffi.

Ils prirent peur tous les deux et ne cessaient de prier.

— Le seigneur est avec vous, répondit Crédulon. Vois-tu ces hommes transparents comme des fantômes monter et descendre la colline du château ?

— Je vous salue Marie, répondit Bouffi.

Et oui il les voyait, les fantômes, mais n'avait osé répondre que par une prière. Ils étaient effrayés. Et si c'était la vérité qui venait à eux ?

— J'ai peur, dit Crédulon.

— Nous prions la Vierge Marie, répondit l'écho.

Bouffi et Crédulon l'entendaient tous les deux. D'où venons-nous, où allons-nous ? Qui sommes-nous ? Qui le savait ?

Lourd de leur marche, mais en même temps léger grâce aux signes du ciel, bien qu'ils étaient tous les deux effrayés. Ils s'arrêtèrent un instant.

— Levez les mains vers le Dieu trois fois saint ! répondit l'écho.

D'où venons-nous, qui sommes-nous, vers qui marchons nous ? Il y avait plus d'un fantôme, et aussi une Dame Blanche. Ils ne savaient pas s'ils rêvaient ou si c'était la réalité. Maintenant qu'ils avaient vu la Dame Blanche, ils se sentirent apaisés.

Il était 15 h 07.

Et le petit train arrivait en transportant trente-trois personnes. Ils entendirent :

— C'est nous ses amis. Nous sommes le corps.

— Le corps du Christ ! répondit l'écho.

Un nuage donna un dégradé de lumière au soleil. Le ciel bleu retentissait. La foule des vivants comme des morts se trouva réunie.

— Vive la vie ! répondit l'écho.

Bouffi et Crédulon redescendirent la colline du château et se rendirent à la cathédrale Sainte Réparate, Place Rossetti.

Là, ils allumèrent un cierge et remercièrent le bon Dieu pour cette étrange et belle expérience.

Depuis ce jour, ils prièrent beaucoup la Vierge Marie et l'été suivant ils partirent en pèlerinage à Lourdes.

Karolina Bonde remercie vivement sa mère et sa sœur pour leurs encouragements et Angélique Kasse pour la correction orthographique.

Les aventures de Rosine Delfeuille

Prélude

La sonnerie venait de retentir. La bouilloire près du grille-pain sifflait fort. Elle terminait sa tartine à la confiture de mûre, les mûres du jardin, pas de la gelée de supermarché. Elle le voyait comme un luxe, si futile soit-il. Celui-ci, elle se l'accordait. Elle le pouvait. Le tracteur dans le champ de blé voisin ne venait pas perturber sa tranquillité. Au contraire, bercée, elle écoutait sa chanson préférée. Elle se remémorait le pourquoi du comment ou ces derniers mois si déroutants, si ambitieux peut-être dans un certain sens. Elle avait décidé, entremêlées, diverses choses. Divers tournants qui devaient changer son cadre et ses habitudes. Elle avait quitté son mari ou plutôt n'était pas retournée au sein du foyer conjugal après une énième dispute. Elle savait qu'il s'agissait de violences conjugales. Sa gynécologue, son alliée depuis des années, avait parlé pour elle. Elle le savait depuis longtemps, si longtemps, mais quelle date, en fait elle avait beau chercher, elle ne se le rappelait pas. Toute à ses pensées, son attention fut quelque peu détournée par un élément voisin, un bruit.

Aventures

Elle était confortablement installée sur sa terrasse. Il faut dire que son luxe de confiture n'influait pas sur celui de la taille de son appartement. Assez petit mais de taille convenable pour l'accueillir elle et ses enfants, elle ne s'en plaignait pourtant pas. Elle ne se plaignait guère tout court d'ailleurs.

Raisonnable, tel aurait pu être son credo. Elle avait fait en sorte de s'y tenir et pourtant au fond d'elle, au plus profond, un feu ardent crépitait, une envie de tellement plus. Ses ambitions déboutées avaient un goût d'inachevé. Elle le savait. Elle revoyait les images d'elle en hôtesse de l'air. Elle souriait face à cette photographie d'elle mannequin. Elle avait si durement jugé ses années d'adolescence. Elle avait été si embêtée ou du moins portait ce ressentiment de l'enfance. Son entrée à l'âge adulte, tout au contraire, ou plutôt son arrivée au lycée avait balayé toute cela. Des études et une licence plus tard, de nombreux flirts, elle n'avait que l'embarras du choix entre ses prétendants qui ne lui résistaient que très rarement.

Elle, qui n'avait pas l'habitude des ratés, aurait dû se douter que ses nombreux repêchages à l'examen de personnel navigant commercial ne présageait pas le meilleur dans cette profession. Elle avait finalement été retenue par une compagnie aérienne parisienne et une autre anglaise. Elle avait privilégié la seconde option. Elle ne savait pas exactement pourquoi. Elle multipliait les vols courts sur une journée plutôt que d'accumuler des moyens ou longs courriers. C'est toute à ses réflexions qu'elle se leva de sa chaise longue où elle s'était confortablement installée. La chaise en joli bois reflétait comme le reste du mobilier du bon goût de son habitante. Sa sœur était d'ailleurs décoratrice. C'était, là encore, un point qui ne l'avait pas épargnée. Elle se sentait lésée ou tellement moins performante professionnellement que ses frères et sœur. Une sœur responsable d'une boutique de décoration, un frère occupant un haut poste dans l'armée au service des achats servant à la défense du pays et un frère ainé, chef connu en Australie disposant de plusieurs restaurants.

Connue, était-ce cela qu'elle recherchait ou qui lui avait manqué ? Certainement pas, c'était moins le fait d'être connue que reconnue qui nourrissait sa peine et son sentiment de futilité voire presque d'inutilité.

Ses enfants auraient pu la contredire peut-être mais la petite enfance n'est pas la plus propice à l'objectivité ou la reconnaissance transgénérationnelle.

Elle se leva. Elle se tourna sans se douter que presque tout allait basculer cet après-midi-là. Elle vit cette femme tenant un couteau à la main. Elle ne distinguait rien de plus. La femme se rendit compte que son store s'était légèrement déplié mais ne parut pas y prêter une attention particulière. Elle enclencha la fermeture du volet automatique. La soirée n'était pourtant pas amorcée.

Rosine était debout, un peu sciée par l'image dont elle venait d'être témoin.

Elle ne le savait pas encore mais c'est son sens de l'observation et sa perspicacité qui devraient lui faire découvrir cette première énigme au sein de la vallée verte.

Elle enfila sa jupe portefeuille, laissée pendante à son transat. Elle y était tout à son aise. Blanche ou colorée, à imprimés ou unie, elle était sa pièce de dressing favorite. Sa préférence allait à celle d'un vert émeraude. Il rappelait la couleur de son iris. Elle avait gardé de son expérience dans la mode, un goût certain pour le choix de ses tenues. Une secrétaire avait tout autant le droit qu'une avocate ou une cadre de s'habiller de façon remarquable. Il s'agissait là du sens littéral du mot. Rosine était de celles qui aimait être remarquée, aimée. Une psychanalyste lui aurait certainement rapproché son enfance chaotique mais elle était à mille lieues de souhaiter une psychanalyse analytique de sa personne. Elle accordait davantage de crédit aux psychothérapeutes comportementalistes.

Son intuition la trompait rarement. Son intuition venait de lui dicter un meurtre. Aussi déconcertant que cela pouvait paraître, elle s'appuyait sur le couteau, du bruit entendu et de l'expression du visage de sa voisine. Elle était fine observatrice. Elle se souhaitait fine psychologue. Le volet fermé, l'image restée intacte dans la tête de la demoiselle de trente et un ans. Elle savait qu'elle était riche de son expérience. Elle avait étudié. Elle avait voyagé. Elle avait travaillé. Elle avait tissé de grandes amitiés. Ce qui avait pu froisser ce tableau idyllique était la perte de son premier bébé. Elle avait donné naissance quelques mois après à son fils. Suivait une fille quatre ans plus tard.

Fraîchement divorcée, elle pensait pouvoir se reposer dans son jardin entre une journée de travail et la garde de ses enfants.

C'était sans compter sur son voisinage.

Elle s'était pensée tranquille mais la résidence privée dans laquelle elle s'était établie quelques mois plus tôt devait se révéler propice à de nombreuses intrigues mystérieuses. À mesure qu'elle y pensait, elle réfléchissait aussi à son propre parcours. Les images s'entremêlaient. Cette élucidation d'un premier mystère devait tout autant l'aider personnellement, dans le plongement et l'acceptation de son effroyable expérience conjugale.

C'est ainsi que devaient débuter les intrigues de mademoiselle Delfeuille !

Souvenirs

S'entremêlaient donc ses souvenirs et ses enquêtes inattendues. Les premiers devaient l'aider à résoudre les secondes. Riche de son expérience personnelle, son esprit vagabondait justement à cet instant jusqu'à son début de relation avec son ex-mari, ou plutôt une histoire un peu cinglée de deux personnes certainement amoureuses mais davantage encore immatures. Et la voilà qui replongeait dans cette soirée en discothèque, une nuit de juin, dix-sept ans plus tôt. Quel était ce secret ? Quel était son secret ? Le savoir, serait-ce révéler une vérité enfouie ? Le révéler brusquerait-il un séisme émotionnel ?

Elle était elle. Elle était telle une multitude d'autres femmes françaises en ce sens. Une victime elle était. Une femme forte elle devenait.

Rosine avait rencontré un amour de folie, un coup de foudre pensait-elle, disait-elle à seize ans. Solweig, sa meilleure amie n'aurait pas dit cela mais peu lui en importait à cette époque. Certains jugeaient cet âge si jeune, d'autres ne s'étonneraient pas de savoir qu'à cet âge de jeunesse et naïveté, une pareille idylle ait pu naître.

Il était à flirter avec une amie à elle. Elle était vierge de toute relation. À peine un baiser avait pu venir balayer sa pureté quelques semaines plus tôt. Fougue du lycée, envie de découverte, elle s'était laissée inviter à cette soirée.

Son amie devait l'initier aux discothèques, aux sorties, à l'alcool et surtout aux rencontres. C'était ce qui devait bercer Rosine, elle si discrète, si secrète jusqu'alors. Alors, Rosine avait bu, un peu. Observé, beaucoup. Dansé, outrageusement. Et accepté les bras du bel amoureux de son amie au moment des slows. Sadie était rentrée. Bien que cela ne soit pas recommandable, Rosine terriblement attirée, n'avait pas pu refuser l'invitation d'Henry.

Cette danse devait la transcender, les transcender, pour plus d'une quinzaine d'années.

Elle avait rêvassé. Elle avait imaginé. Elle avait désiré. Elle avait obtenu. C'était un défi, aussi. Était-ce une obsession peut-être ? Si nombreux étaient les termes qui auraient pu définir ses pensées après cette danse envoûtante.

Rentrée chez elle, cette sensation de boule au ventre ne devait pas disparaître des jours durant. Alors qu'elle s'envolait rendre visite à une amie à la montagne en Haute-Savoie, la curiosité du jeune garçon elle aussi s'était accentuée.

Il attendait son retour et la rejoignait très vite, non loin de chez ses parents. Il lui proposait une promenade en bord de mer, comme elle les aimait tant.

Il était en couple pourtant. Un message de son téléphone portable à Sadie balayait sa précédente courte relation avec elle. Cette base, plutôt insolite, aurait pu laisser présager du rythme proche de montagnes russes des années suivantes. Elle ne le laissait pas s'échapper, s'envoler. Sa pugnacité était née. Était-ce une conséquence de sa première meilleure amie qui l'avait laissée, de ses parents qui ne l'avaient pas entendue ? Était-ce son caractère qui s'affirmait finalement ? Peut-être bien, certainement lui me protégerait se disait-elle. Cette envie de lui, comme elle avait besoin de lui.

Rosine avait besoin. Elle avait besoin de l'amour, un besoin quasi insatiable. C'était à l'image d'une quête, d'un bonheur inabouti.

Elle rentrait en terminale et devait affronter le regard de l'ex-amie de son amoureux. Elle se sentait pourtant forte d'un amour insubmersible même si elle avait réalisé dès les premières semaines qu'Henry était différent des autres garçons, fuyant.

Elle lui avait offert sa virginité. Il lui avait prise assez sauvagement. Finalement, leurs interprétations étaient si différentes mais il lui faudrait des années pour le comprendre, l'accepter.

Ainsi, en ce début d'année, à l'aube de sa majorité, il la quittait. Il la déposait devant chez ses parents où elle habitait encore. Telle une petite chose fragile, elle se recroquevillait. Un jeu qui allait s'avérer sanglant était amorcé. Sa seule préoccupation était qu'il l'appelle. Qu'il l'appelle, encore et encore. Elle ne lâchait pas son téléphone portable. Elle ne cessait de le dessiner, de le chérir, de l'aimer.

Il l'appelait finalement un soir mais la mineure se voyait refuser la sortie par ses parents. Alors, elle cessa pratiquement de s'alimenter. Elle cessait d'aimer. Elle abandonnait toute sortie, se plongeait somme toute dans les livres. La littérature ou la musique, l'art en général et même des dissertations de philosophie lui permettaient seulement d'oublier un peu, tel un alcool qui enivre. L'été arrivait et elle obtenait son diplôme. Alors, elle se repris en main. Elle resplendissait. Une pugnacité apparaissait. Il était hors de question qu'elle ne se fane. Son espoir était inébranlable. Il était tel la rose rouge, sa fleur favorite.

Retour à l'enquête

La jeune femme voisine devait avoir trente ans pensait-elle. Elle faisait le parallèle avec elle-même facilement quelques années auparavant, souvenir de la violence de la relation toxique avec le père de ses enfants. Un soulagement la parcourut et pour elle, et pour cette femme, qui vraisemblablement n'avait pas d'enfant avec son concubin qui ne paraissait être violent qu'envers elle. Était-elle du signe scorpion elle aussi ?

Rosine était coupée dans ses pensées par sa voisine de palier, Anastasie. Tout son opposé mais aussi fortement présente, elle lui accordait toute sa confiance. Elle la remercia pour le plat qu'elle venait de lui concocter et rentrait le mettre au réfrigérateur.

De sa fenêtre, elle entrevoyait les rideaux de l'appartement de sa jeune voisine en face. Entre leur jonction, la lame du couteau était visible. Plus tôt, elle avait assisté à des scènes de ménage entre les tourtereaux, terme qui se révélait plutôt inapproprié finalement. Rosine se demanda si elle devait intervenir. Mais quel était son rôle ? Ceci devait définir sa position dans chacune de ses enquêtes futures.

Rosine ne savait pas très bien se situer dans le sens où elle avait presque un don infaillible pour reconnaître une victime mais bien souvent, elle trouvait des circonstances atténuantes au coupable. Elle savait que cela devait changer pourtant. Cette fois, elle se remémorait les allers et venues du mari de la jeune résidente. Lui-même avait dû maintes et maintes fois avoir l'occasion de menacer sa femme à en croire le ton qu'il employait lors de leurs disputes. Un instant, elle se dit que son devoir était de prévenir la police mais avant même qu'elle n'ait pu attraper le téléphone, une autre idée lui vint, meilleure de toute évidence selon elle.

Lentement, elle fit le tour de son modeste jardin. Alors qu'elle franchissait le portail de la bâtisse annexe, le rideau de l'appartement de la jeune femme avait déjà été refermé.

Rosine sonnait. Personne ne vint lui ouvrir. Elle attendait patiemment. Finalement, un voisin apparut. Elle se faufilait discrètement derrière lui, dans le vaste hall de l'entrée. Cet immeuble était de toute évidence très différent et plus ancien que le sien. Des poutres apparentes au plafond ainsi qu'aux murs laissaient entendre qu'un seul léger plancher en bois devait séparer les appartements aux différents étages. Elle se disait que le bruit de la scène de laquelle elle avait été témoin avait dû être ressenti par l'ensemble des résidents de l'immeuble quoique l'horaire, 15 heures, promettait à la victime un certain isolement, si tant est que la femme ou l'homme habitant cet appartement quatre se figurait être une victime. En effet, Rosine avait deviné le numéro du logement qu'elle recherchait, selon le plan d'évacuation jauni, affiché tout près de l'ascenseur vieillot, aux lourdes portes métalliques, rappelant le Paris Haussmannien.

Elle attendit le clic du monte-charge qui venait de redescendre. Elle s'y enferma et referma d'un coup sec la lourde grille dorée. Si Rosine était tenace, elle n'en était pas moins pétrifiée de gravir ces étages sans savoir réellement ce qu'elle y trouverait. Elle prit une grande inspiration alors qu'elle quittait presque à regret l'ascenseur grinçant.

Elle avait imaginé essuyer un refus de l'occupante alors qu'elle frapperait à sa porte. Mais rien de tout cela, l'entrée était même entrouverte. Elle prit son courage à deux mains et tourna la poignée ronde couleur or, fidèle au style décoratif de la bâtisse. Elle longea un corridor puis un deuxième. De l'extérieur, elle n'aurait pas pu se douter que l'immeuble pouvait prétendre à de si vastes appartements. Elle zigzaguait à travers et cela lui parut presque tout aussi long que le trajet effectué depuis chez elle. Soudain, elle la vit. La femme était là, devant elle, figée. Telle une statue, elle se tenait droite, presque à se confondre avec la tapisserie pâle qui ornait le haut mur. Vêtue d'une robe légère de saison couleur abricot, elle était proche d'un reflet qu'aurait pu renvoyer le rideau derrière elle.

Le couteau était maintenant posé sur une petite table blanche dont le dessus, une large coupelle en verre, ne réussissait pas à absorber les gouttes de sang rejetées par la lame. Le goutte-à-goutte qui filait de la hauteur de la tablette, au plancher en bois épais, faillit presque faire défaillir Rosine. Elle se reprit, fermement décidée à élucider ce mystère si proche et qui pourtant lui apparaissait comme un sac de nœuds à dénouer.

Elle se demanda comment aurait réagi sa voisine Anastasie. Elle avait tendance à douter d'elle-même. Un furieux manque de confiance en elle l'empêchait souvent d'aller au fond de ses envies mais pas cette fois. Elle était motivée à obtenir la confiance et la confidence de cette voisine. Encore sous le traumatisme de son ex-mari, elle savait combien l'entourage, une main ou une écoute bienveillante pouvait permettre de soulager toute personne en proie à une détresse terrible telle que semblait présenter l'habitante de l'appartement doré.

Elle avait donné ce nom à ce dernier. Chacun des logements avait un numéro qui permettait à son propriétaire ou à son locataire de disposer d'une place de parking attitrée. Mais Rosine, poète, avait trouvé tout naturellement plus amusant de les renommer par couleur.

Elle remarquait dans l'angle de la pièce où elles se trouvaient, un fauteuil aux coussins d'un bleu profond. Un ours en peluche était posé dessus. Il représentait le caractère encore juvénile de la jeune fille se disait-elle. À peine la bougie couleur cerise allumée sur la jolie étagère juste au-dessus lui faisait revenir à la véritable raison de sa présence en ce lieu.

Le nounours beige lui évoquait un souvenir, celui de son ex conjoint qui la punissait, lui cassant des objets. Elle se réfugiait alors dans l'une des vastes chambres de leur demeure sous les combles et y serrait fort son Teddy bear.

Une senteur exotique parcourait la pièce et il vint à Rosine une évidence quant à l'identité du coupable présumé de ce qui devait devenir sa première enquête.

Mi sueño

J'ai encore rêvé de toi cette nuit. Comment lui avouer, à lui qui s'endort à mes côtés chaque soir, qu'une fois l'obscurité tombée je n'aspire qu'à te retrouver.

Certes, il te ressemble un peu physiquement et c'est très certainement ce qui a motivé mon choix. Son teint basané, ses cheveux foncés mi-longs et soyeux qu'il attache en queue-de-cheval, ses yeux noir brillant me perçant du regard et son sourire dévastateur m'ont tout de suite plu chez lui.

Mais je criais déjà à la chimère à notre rencontre. Il n'a ni ton timbre de voix, ni l'emprise que tu as sur moi.

Depuis mes quinze ans, tu hantes mes nuits. Je peux presque sentir tes mains sur mon corps durant mon sommeil. Je perçois tes baisers sur ma peau innocente, un mélange subtil de caresses brûlantes et de luxure.

Encore ce matin au réveil, je prie pour que mes gémissements n'aient éveillé ses soupçons durant mon orgasme nocturne.

J'ai beaucoup de tendresse pour lui et au fil des ans, des sentiments ont vu le jour. Je m'en voudrais terriblement de le faire souffrir de cette façon. J'essaie de me convaincre qu'il ne s'agit en aucun cas d'une relation incestueuse. Tu n'es qu'un songe après tout. J'ai besoin de toi, tu me procures force et apaisement.

Lorsqu'une situation me semble difficilement surmontable, c'est en toi que je viens puiser ma détermination. J'ai longtemps cru voir en toi un idéal masculin, un super héros qui veillerait sur moi dans l'ombre. Je pensais qu'un jour tu disparaîtrais avec le temps ou avec les cadeaux que la vie m'octroierait. Je n'en suis plus sûre. En fait, à l'heure actuelle, je ne suis plus sûre de rien.

Plus les années passent, plus tu manques à ma vie et là où d'autres personnes se réfugient dans l'addiction, tu restes la mienne.

Je prends une douche rapide avant de partir au travail.

Nécessaire, entre les mauvaises nouvelles de la veille et la chaleur avec laquelle tu m'as réconforté toute la nuit.

Il se peut que je doive licencier du personnel, la pandémie débutante ayant décimé une bonne partie de la patientèle de ma société. Tu ne sembles pas d'accord, tu me demande de patienter, tu me sermonne à nouveau. Si posé, si intelligent et toujours de bon conseil, mon cœur te suivrait jusqu'au bout du monde mais mon esprit cartésien doit se résigner. Jouer la santé financière de mon entreprise sur un rêve, c'est un bien gros pari. Je commencerais par diminuer mon propre horaire de travail.

Depuis quelques temps une idée fixe me hantait, mais le temps me manquait. Écrire un livre sur nous, sur la relation que nous entretenons depuis toutes ces années. Bien évidemment, je broderais le récit, rendant l'histoire plus captivante pour le lecteur.

Je mêlerais toutefois à l'intrigue une part de vérité. Je te décrirais, tel que tu m'apparais en rêve. Hormis les précisions physiques apportées plus haut, je ne manquerais pas de mentionner tes traits de caractère. Tes sautes d'humeur impromptus, tes colères dont toi seul en connaît la cause, ton sens de l'humour sarcastique, ainsi que le besoin de t'isoler quand tu es tracassé.

Je rentrais plus tôt ce midi et comme à mon habitude, je checkais mes mails sur le chemin du retour. Une offre d'emploi pour Puerto Rico. Un sourire se dessina sur mon visage. Pourquoi ne pas débuter mon roman par ce genre de décision. Je pourrais y inclure les paysages que tu me montres en rêve, je savais vers quelle destination guider mes recherches.

Il manquait toutefois quelque chose de crucial à mon récit, il me fallait te donner une identité. Les petits noms que je te donnais durant nos ébats ne suffiraient pas à attiser la curiosité de nos lecteurs. Je décidais donc, me prenant au jeu, que tu allais m'aider. Je laissais s'écouler les matins, retranscrivant chaque sensation que tu me faisais ressentir la nuit durant. Je m'éveillais brusquement cette nuit-là, m'asseyant sur mon lit comme frappée par la foudre.

« Antonio ! » m'écriais-je avant de retomber dans une torpeur presque instantanée.

Les semaines passaient, le bouquin avançait doucement mais le travail extérieur stagnait. Ma collègue me pressait un peu plus chaque jour pour prendre une décision. Difficile de lui confier que mon amant imaginaire me parle d'une future association avec une collègue souffrant de problèmes cardiaques. Bien que fort compréhensive, je l'entendais déjà me conseiller de consulter.

« Si tu veux partir, attends ! » me répétais-tu sans cesse.

Mes nuits agitées me forçaient à m'assoupir l'après-midi.

Laissant défiler le fil d'actualité de Facebook et sentant le sommeil m'envahir, je tombais sur une demande de remplacement d'une collègue. Je m'empressais de lui envoyer un message afin comprendre sa démarche. En arrêt forcé par son cardiologue, elle quémandait une aide urgente sur les réseaux professionnels.

La nouvelle me glaça le sang. Bien qu'elle envisagea une réaction empathique de ma part, mon attitude ne reflétait que la stupéfaction engendrée par la coïncidence. Moins d'une semaine plus tard, sa patientèle venait agrandir la nôtre, garantissant de la sorte l'emploi de ma collègue.

Tout rentrait progressivement dans l'ordre, mais mon esprit s'évadait de plus en plus. J'étais distraite, je présentais des difficultés à me concentrer. Il m'arrivait de sourire bêtement, sans aucune raison et sans m'en rendre compte. Mon entourage me le fit vite remarquer.

Idem au travail, quand vous êtes de nature perfectionniste, une telle conduite ne passe pas inaperçue. Je ne trouvais plus d'échappatoire et me confiais à ma collègue. Je lui parlais de mes rêves, sans pour autant rentrer dans les détails et de l'aboutissement qui en découlais. Elle m'écouta attentivement.

« Ce n'est pas tout », surenchérissais-je.

Plus j'élargissais mes recherches dans l'élaboration de mon manuscrit, plus le sentiment de « déjà vu » m'envahissait. C'est une aperception qu'elle connaissait. Ce n'était pas la première fois qu'elle la ressentait.

« Oui, moi aussi, cette sensation d'avoir été témoin ou d'avoir déjà vécu une situation présente, accompagnée d'irréalité ne m'était pas inconnue. Je l'avais étudié en cours de neurologie. Il s'agit d'une forme de paramnésie, et si je ne m'abuse, cette impression touche à peu près septante-cinq pourcent de la population. Probablement lié à ton stress... » me réconforta-t-elle.

Elle n'avait peut-être pas totalement tort, mais je ne m'expliquais toujours pas le fait de rêver d'endroits précis en étant totalement certaine de ne jamais les avoir visités. Je me résonnais et me replongeais dans le labeur de mes interminables journées. Je terminais fréquemment vers vingt heures, à quelques rues de mon domicile par une dame assez âgée et très dépendante déléguée par ma collègue souffrante.

D'origine italienne mais parlant un français parfait, nous avions en commun la passion de la lecture. Je passais un peu plus de temps à ses côtés, essayant de briser un peu sa solitude. Nous faisions chaque jour plus ample connaissance.

Bien qu'happée par mon travail, mon attention se détourna vers le poste de télévision allumé sur la chaîne italienne. Des applaudissements retentissaient après chaque présentation des candidats d'un jeu télévisé.

« Antonio », entendais-je.

Bien évidemment, c'est un nom à consonance italienne, pensais-je. Je me pétrifiais. Mes mains se mirent à trembler. La patiente me fit remarquer la pâleur de mon visage. Sa voix résonnait dans le lointain. J'eus un flash-back digne d'un film de sciences fiction. La même phrase retentissait dans ma tête... un nom à consonance italienne.

« Assieds-toi un instant, tu dois être fatiguée », me conseilla la dame.

Absorbée par mes pensées, je lui souris.

Je me hâtais de clôturer mes soins et ne tardais pas à prendre congé. Je me réfugiais dans ma voiture et m'écroulais sur le volant.

« Mais qu'est-ce qu'il m'arrive », m'interrogeais-je paniquée.

Je me remémorais un souvenir enfui dans mon esprit datant de quelques années auparavant.

Nous devions être en été, un peu avant mes vacances annuelles. Je travaillais seule en cette période, ma collègue étant déjà en repos. Je bouquinais tranquillement allongée sur mon lit, me délassant d'une longue journée de travail. Le téléphone retentit me provoquant un léger sursaut. Le service de garde des urgences policières recherchait un prestataire de soins. Je pris de quoi noter, lui demandant de patienter un instant. Il insista sur la particularité de sa démarche. Je l'écoutais, griffonnant sur le bloc note. Un patient étranger, se débrouillant très peu en français avait besoin de soins urgent. Je regardais l'heure tardive en haut de l'écran de mon smartphone. Bien que le soleil ne se soit encore couché, la paresse et la fatigue me firent soupirer.

« Il serait plus sage de le guider vers l'hôpital le plus proche », conseillais-je au policier.

Là était le problème, le jeune garçon y avait été refusé faute de couverture sociale. Je soupirais à nouveau, « qu'Hippocrate se retourne dans sa tombe ! » grognais-je, blasée de cette société matérialiste où l'empathie ne trouvait plus sa place.

« Donnez-moi l'adresse », demandais-je en me rendant au rez-de-chaussée dans le but de me préparer à reprendre la route.

« Vous ne serez pas payée », insista à nouveau mon interlocuteur.

« Ça ne m'empêchera pas de dormir », lui assurais-je.

Il me renseigna un parking situé à une distance d'environ deux kilomètres de ma résidence.

« SDF ? » m'informais-je.

« Non, gens du voyage », précisa-t-il.

Je restais silencieuse.

« Un problème ? » me questionna-t-il brisant mon mutisme.

« Non », murmurais-je.

Adepte des films d'horreur, je ne connaissais de la culture tzigane que ce que le petit écran reflétait. Je priais le soleil d'attendre un peu avant de disparaître de l'horizon.

J'arrivais à vive allure vers ma destination. Je n'eus à chercher, me dirigeant vers un amas de caravanes disposées en quinconce. Je slalomais entre les remorques et roulottes à vitesse réduite, attendant d'être interpellée par un passant. Malgré les nombreux regards jetés sur mon véhicule, personne ne s'approcha. Je pris sur moi de descendre pour demander mon chemin. Je m'approchais d'une dame, occupée à étendre son linge sur une corde tirée entre un auvent et le toit du camping-car. Juste un bonsoir de ma part lui suffit à prendre la fuite.

« OK, c'est pas gagné », murmurais-je, cherchant du regard une autre personne susceptible de me répondre.

Une tente plus imposante trônait un peu plus loin et quelques hommes y gravitaient. Je me sentais dévisagée et un sentiment de malaise commençait à m'envahir peu à peu. Je pris la carte imprimée de mon caducée dans la voiture. Un langage universel pourrait aider à briser la glace. Je me dirigeais dans leur direction, brandissant ma carte comme une guerrière se protégeant derrière un bouclier. La métaphore me fit sourire. Un homme très grand et costaud s'approcha de moi. Sa chemise à carreau ouverte laissait apercevoir sa pilosité entremêlée à une large chaîne dorée. Deux grands anneaux d'or lui transperçaient chaque oreille. Mal rasé et les cheveux longs bouclés lui descendant sur les épaules appuyaient mes stéréotypes. Il me fit signe de le suivre. Je m'exécutais timidement. Mon air craintif le fit sourire d'une impeccable dentition blanche.

Il m'emmena dans une caravane blanche semblant flambant neuve. Un jeune homme y était allongé sur un lit, en position fœtale. Sa posture m'indiquait une douleur intense ressentie. Une dame d'une cinquantaine d'années accroupie lui épongeait le front avec un linge qu'elle replongeait aussitôt dans une bassine jonchant le sol. Le visage déformé par sa souffrance, il me fixa un instant avant de s'adresser à sa mère dans une langue complètement incompréhensible pour moi. Elle se leva et sorti de l'habitacle, nous laissant seul le jeune homme et moi. Il déboutonna son pantalon et le baissa effectuant difficilement un retournement complet de son corps. Une énorme tâche transperçait son caleçon. Le tissu fusionnait à la plaie. Je pris le linge humide de la bassine pour le décoller en douceur. Un abcès avait percé, voir explosé. Une cavité béante purulente creusait la moitié de sa fesse. Je commençais à irriguer la plaie à l'aide d'une seringue et d'une solution physiologique.

Ne pouvant communiquer, ne connaissant le risque allergique, j'optais pour un traitement local neutre, méchant l'intégralité du cratère avec des compresses imprégnées d'un corps gras. Mon soin terminé, je tentais un langage de signes. Je mimais une prise de médicaments par la bouche. Il me montra une boîte dans une armoire. D'une provenance étrangère, je scrutais la composition des comprimés. Souvent traduites du latin, les molécules peuvent facilement se reconnaître. Penicillium. Je levais le pouce en guise d'approbation.

Je fis un mouvement avec les mains se croisant l'une par-dessus l'autre, lui demandant s'il ne prenait rien d'autre. Il répondit négativement de la tête. Je fouillais ma mallette à la recherche d'antidouleurs et lui remis une plaquette d'échantillon. Je lui indiquais la posologie avec les doigts. D'un signe de la main je le saluais, lui signalant d'une part mon départ et ma visite du lendemain.

Le lendemain, je lui rendais visite en fin de tournée. J'eus un peu de mal à le reconnaître, assis autour d'une table avec d'autres adolescents, il semblait moins algique que la veille.

Je lui donnais dix-sept, dix-huit ans, pas au-delà. Il se leva à mon arrivée, très mince et plus grand que moi, il me précéda. J'entendis un grognement qui le fit s'arrêter brusquement. Il se retourna vers une vieille dame qui semblait dormir sur une chaise à bascule qui devait avoir le même âge qu'elle. Les yeux fermés à peine visible derrière de longs cheveux gris lui couvrant un visage flétrit par le temps, elle grommela une phrase semblant sortie d'outre-tombe.

De la première marche de la remorque, il me fixa de ses yeux aussi noirs que le charbon, le visage souriant, il passa une main dans ses cheveux.

« Tu parles espagnol », me dit-il en riant.

Je le fixais interrogative. Comment pouvait-il le savoir. Enfin, soit, nous avions enfin trouvé un moyen de communiquer.

Je dû le soigner durant un mois. Son jeune âge lui donnant une capacité à cicatriser très vite.

Plus les jours passaient, plus il me semblait que les gens se montraient accueillants, plus souriants. Ils saluaient mon passage. Les mères laissaient leurs enfants m'approcher. Certaines femmes venaient me demander des conseils médicaux. Ils m'offraient chaque jour une boisson fraîche que je n'osais refuser. Je fus même invitée à un barbecue familial mais je déclinais poliment l'invitation prétextant un souper prévu avec mon mari.

Durant presque un mois, la vieille dame au visage ridé ne semblait avoir bougé d'un millimètre. Toujours vêtue des mêmes haillons, je la fixais parfois pour voir si elle respirait encore. Elle se remit à grogner en baragouinant à nouveau une sorte d'incantation. Me sentant fixée par l'entourage, je m'informais sur la nature de ses paroles. Ils se mirent à rire, « elle dit que c'est faux, tu n'es pas mariée. »

J'hochais la tête.

« Depuis toutes ces années, c'est la même chose. Nous vivons maritalement », me confessais-je.

Elle grogna à nouveau.

« Elle dit que c'est pas la même chose », me traduirent-ils à nouveau.

Elle se leva, rien que la voir bouger me pétrifia.

Elle s'avança vers moi. Je me sentais sur le qui-vive, prête à bondir vers elle, anticipant sa chute. Lentement elle se positionna face à moi et saisi ma main.

Sa petite stature m'obligeait à baisser les yeux. La déformation de sa colonne vertébrale me donnait l'impression qu'elle gardait la forme de son fauteuil. Elle fixait ma main gauche, glissant ses doigts crochus à l'intérieur. Ses ongles longs et ébréchés me chatouillaient. Elle leva son regard vers moi. Me terrifia d'un œil noir luisant, tandis que je ne pouvais me détourner de l'autre cavité orbitaire renfermant un œil de verre terne et visqueux. Elle me sourit, laissant apparaître une dentition parsemée de couronne d'or.

« Si elle m'arrache un bouton, je suis foutue », pensais-je, repensant à un film d'horreur.

Elle commença à parler. Je me retournais vers mon patient.

« Je ne comprends rien », lui murmurais-je.

« Elle te fait un cadeau, pour te remercier. »

« Chut ! » s'exclama-t-elle.

Elle reprit, mais cette fois, en espagnol.

« Je vois un homme, un nom à consonance italienne. »

Je la laissais poursuivre, pensant, aucune chance, ça ne m'attire pas trop les italiens.

Elle leva le regard : « Je n'ai jamais dit qu'il était italien ! »

Je levais les sourcils, elle a lu dans mes pensées, c'est impossible.

« Il n'est pas italien », m'affirma-t-elle.

« Antonio ! Et je te vois entourée de filles. »

« Raté, me flaquais-je à rire. J'ai eu deux garçons. »

Elle se mit à rire à son tour.

« Pourquoi crois-tu que tu achètes toutes ses poupées ? »

Je sursautais. Mais comment...

« Maintenant tais-toi ! » me gronda-t-elle.

Elle ne levait plus les yeux.

« Tu as dévié de ta trajectoire à cause de ta mère. »

« Elle est décédée », lui confiais-je avec tristesse.

Elle acheva : « tu dois retourner à ton point de départ et tu retrouveras ta destinée. »

Elle me confia d'autres choses... que je garderai pour moi pour l'instant.

Je parti en la remerciant, mais ne prêtant aucune attention à ses révélations.

Le lendemain, je me présentais comme à l'habitude, mais le parking était désert. Ils étaient partis, sans laisser une quelconque trace de leur passage et sans même avoir dit au revoir.

Je me relevais du volant, comme groggy après un cauchemar. Je me sentais comme au centre d'un puzzle, qu'on complétait enfin des dernières pièces manquantes. Mais une chose était indéniable, pour la première fois depuis longtemps, j'étais certaine d'être là où je devais et au moment voulu, quel que soit la force qui m'y avait poussé.

« Quel point de départ ? Je ne comprends plus rien, je vais devenir folle ! » balbutiais-je à voix haute.

Je revoyais ma mère malade. Ses larmes quand je lui ai annoncé l'arrêt de mes études de médecine pour prendre soin d'elle.

Son envie de connaître ses petits enfants avant de partir. Ma tentative ayant de toute façon échoué. Son décès le jour de la naissance de mon fils. J'écarquillais les yeux, je devais partir pour l'Amérique latine avec une œuvre humanitaire.

J'attrapais mon smartphone sur le siège passager, je n'avais pas effacé mes contacts malgré les années passées. Un peu tard pour appeler, mais j'essayerai dès le lendemain.

Quelques mois se sont écoulés depuis. Le manuscrit a été envoyé à la maison d'édition de mon premier et unique choix.

Grâce à Novum, il prendra vie au début 2022.

Je suis certaine qu'il jouera une pièce maîtresse dans la réalisation de ma destinée. J'ai lu plusieurs ouvrages de physique quantique. Certaines théories y traitant des énergies pouvant expliquer le phénomène qu'on appelle « DESTINÉE ».

J'ai signé un contrat de deux ans dans l'humanitaire pour l'Amérique latine. J'ai repris des cours de langue, une révision d'espagnol et d'anglais. Avec ces deux modules acquits, je compte me rendre à Puerto Rico.

À l'heure actuelle, je pars du principe que mieux vaut vivre avec des remords que des regrets. J'aime entendre dans ta bouche qu'il n'y a pas de hasard et que tout n'est que la volonté de Dieu.

Je me sens l'héroïne du livre de ma vie, je m'endors chaque nuit tournant une page merveilleuse sachant qu'avant la fin du dernier chapitre je connaîtrai enfin l'identité de mon super héros.

Je prie que les étoiles nous donnent assez de temps pour nous retrouver, bien que je ne sois pressée. Commencer un livre par la fin, n'a aucun intérêt !

La femme allongée de la Sainte Victoire

Éléments importants à savoir pour apprécier cette histoire à sa juste valeur : Il faut se rendre en quelques endroits précis, certains villages du pays provençal qui permettent de l'observer : Mimet, Saint Savournin, Gréasque, Fuveau, Rousset, Peynier (et peut-être même d'autres que je n'ai jamais remarqués) sont les noms qui les désignent. Dépassées ces limites, elle devient invisible.

« Il était une fois, en des temps anciens, très reculés sur notre terre, vivaient des géants... » Cette idée peut paraître fantaisiste, certainement infantile. Mais regardons les choses avec un peu plus d'imagination, voire de clairvoyance.

D'une part, nul n'est en mesure de prouver le contraire... Et d'autre part, depuis ma plus tendre enfance, je la voyais en ouvrant les volets de ma chambre.

Elle était là, devant moi, à quelques kilomètres de distance. Je la contemplais chaque jour de l'année avec une sensation différente, une approche différente. Une vision globale similaire, certes.

Mais avec des détails apparaissant, disparaissant au gré des minutes qui s'égrènent, la journée passant, les jeux de lumière et d'ombre s'y reflétant, le moindre nuage pouvant complètement lui donner un air singulier, qui lui-même changera au prochain rayon de soleil levant.

Des fois verte et sauvage, presque forestière.

Des fois rouge ocre, presque jaune solaire.

Des fois gris foncée, presque noire colère !

Très souvent grise bleutée presque couleur de la mer et dont la longueur des cheveux atteint plusieurs centaines de mètres. Elle est là, allongée depuis des milliers d'années.

Cette montagne de Provence rendue célèbre par Paul Cézanne, celle que je porte dans mon cœur : « La Sainte Victoire » possède en son sommet la preuve visible de la théorie sur le gigantisme. Laissons-nous porter pour découvrir ce qu'elle nous réserve.

D'une part, où elle se situe, c'est-à-dire à presque mille mètres d'altitude.

Et d'autre part, de façon plus spirituelle, pour l'apercevoir vraiment une première fois. Car après l'avoir vue, il nous sera possible de regarder la Sainte-Victoire sans la revoir. Elle apparaitra à vos yeux comme elle m'apparait depuis toujours. Enfin... d'aussi loin que je me souvienne.

Tel une découverte vous apercevez tour à tour, sa tête, son front, son nez, son menton, sa volupté qui lui donne un air si charnel. Sa poitrine si féminine de la taille d'une colline qui prédomine. Son ventre est plat jusqu'à ses jambes et, à l'extrémité, on voit parfaitement apparaitre ses pieds, ou plutôt ses bottes de femme, si j'ose dire.

Maintenant, comment ne pas la voir ?! Elle est immense ! Majestueusement belle, mais pas prétentieuse. En harmonie totale avec les éléments. Elle fait partie du paysage. Plus que cela même, c'est elle qui compose le paysage. C'est elle qui le façonne et qui trône en son sommet. Allongée d'une telle façon qu'elle semble attendre le prince charmant qui viendra l'embrasser pour la délivrer de cet état de pierre.

Cet état par lequel elle est quasiment immortelle et qui la laisse figée pour l'éternité au sommet d'une montagne. Et si les géants étaient nos ancêtres, et s'il y a des milliers d'années, le gigantisme était peut-être la simple réalité...

Les dinosaures ayant vécu des millions d'années étaient venus se reproduire et élire domicile aux pieds de « la femme allongée », dans le bassin qui a servi bien plus tard à l'extraction du charbon ; le bassin minier de Provence.

Car aussi gigantesque soit-elle, elle n'en demeure pas moins humaine, saine et naturelle. Elle a couvée au travers du temps des milliers d'habitants, tantôt des hommes et bien plus tôt des Titanosaures.

Depuis tout ce temps, elle dort. Son sommeil serait-il synonyme de tranquillité, prospérité et ... ? Peut-être dort-elle jusqu'à ce que les humains dépassent les bornes afin de recréer la même force utilisée lors de sa création, mais de façon destructrice.

Arrachant à la Sainte Victoire la moitié de son sommet qui compose « la femme allongée ». Pour l'instant, elle est préservée, le massif étant accessible uniquement à pied. Il faut du courage pour parvenir jusqu'à la crête qui dessine les courbes de la douce géante. Plusieurs heures de marches sont nécessaires et le sentier, même banalisé, est déconseillé aux novices. Cela permettra peut-être à sa « vraie nature » d'être conservée...

Dans un flash lointain, je suis à côté de mes parents. Nous regardons par la fenêtre du salon avec désolation, la montagne rouge sang, dans ce début de nuit, le feu s'était emparé d'elle. Je craignais (je trouve cela drôle avec du recul, mais tout de même imaginatif) que les longs cheveux de « la femme allongée » ne brûlent complètement dans l'incendie.

Une grande partie de la montagne avait malheureusement brûlé, mais le lendemain matin, j'ai constaté avec consolation que les cheveux de « la femme allongée » étaient toujours là. Un peu plus ondulés, certes, mais composés de plusieurs mèches descendant en parallèle, comme pour dire « mesdames messieurs, ma chevelure est éternelle ». Voilà de quoi renforcer mes convictions. La sensation que cette femme, cette géante, était une femme que je connaissais et avec laquelle je pouvais laisser libre cours à mon imagination.

C'était un peu comme s'il fallait que je la regarde, pour me sentir rassuré : j'étais et je suis toujours aujourd'hui inexplicablement attiré par elle. Il m'arrive qu'il me tarde de la voir, de l'apprécier, de me laisser me délecter de ce qu'elle déclenche en moi. Comme un pilier indestructible, mais si fragile à la fois.

ELLE ME REMPLIT DE BONHEUR.

Au moment même où j'écris ces phrases, il y a de nouveaux évè-
nements, qui, pour certains, sont preuves d'avenir, d'énergie re-
nouvelable. Et pour d'autres, une aberration qui déchire le paysage. Quoi qu'il en soit, c'est une coïncidence idéale qui vient
étayer mon idée sur la femme allongée. Car ce sont deux parcs
éoliens composés d'immenses hélices productrices d'électrici-
té, qui sont venues s'implanter à quelques contrebas de la vallée qui sert de lit à ma gigantesque amie.

Février fini

Amandiers fleuris

Parmi les tout premiers fleuris,
Parmi aussi les tout derniers à donner leurs fruits,
Les portants presque jusqu'à l'automne...
Blancs, roses violets, sur fond pale bleuté,
Éclat de pétales qui embaument la forêt,
Qui illuminent en bordant les routes de février.
Qui nous rappelle la logique implacable à laquelle
Nous sommes liés :
Pas d'inquiétude les beaux jours sont en train d'arriver !

Poème chevalement magique

Il fût un temps où j'étais vivant, moi le chevalement.
Aujourd'hui en sommeil, ceux qui m'ont connu en leurs descendants,
Tous les 4 décembre me réveillent,
M'illuminent de mille feux pour voir naitre dans leurs yeux les merveilles.
À l'endroit même où se sont noués tant de drames,
Où le charbon a emporté tant d'hommes.
Pour preuves encore la procession de Sainte-barbe,
Celle qui veille sur le mineur,
Et jusqu'au fond du puits l'accompagne.
Construction rivetée, reflet d'une époque,
Armature métallique dressée sur ses longues pattes,
Présent de la Croix de Lorraine jusqu'au soleil de Provence,
Je fus l'étendard, et je reste vestige de charbonnage de France.

Bibliography:
S. 157, 159, 161 © Zenitram

Register

OJOMA IREFU
Ojoma Irefu is a writer, poet, and business owner. Born and raised in Nigeria, Ojoma presently lives in Manchester, United Kingdom where she continues to write poetry, fiction, and non-fiction stories. Irefu can be reached via email at ojomairefu@gmail.com.

ANTHONY R JOHNSON
Born in 1951, Anthony R Johnson was a veterinary surgeon for 42 years, mostly in Crewe. He began writing upon retirement, producing a novel, "There's always a tomorrow", currently being published. Numerous poems, short stories and a children's book have yet to be published.

LORNA MAUREEN MCRAE
Lorna Maureen McRae, from Vancouver, Canada now lives in Calderdale, which she considers an ideal place to live and write. Not quite Vancouver, but history, hills and valleys of inspiration. With a BA in Creative Writing, she enjoys travelling – Canada's west coast, other parts of the Americas and Europe.

LISA MONET
Lisa Monet was born in the Channel Islands but has lived in the south of France since 2004. Having studied languages and literature at university, she now tries to squeeze in writing along with her full-time job and her other interests, music, art, talking to cats/dogs and swimming in the sea.

JW NELSON

JW Nelson writes in multiple genres, from adult comedy drama to poetic pieces for everyone. He writes exciting fiction, adventure stories with ethnically diverse characters interwoven utilising the locality he lives in; Nottinghamshire. He does this whilst passing himself off as a football coach, dancer and Disc Jockey.

SHAMA PERERA

Shama Perera was born in Stockport and brought up in South-West London. She has worked in the corporate world in the city of London for over 20 years. Shama is a mother of three and a writer of screenplays and TV-series. She's also looking to release a children's video game soon.

BEN REUBEN

Ben Reuben went to Highgate School in London. He was diagnosed with a bipolar spectrum mental health disorder in 1980. Since then, he spent 30 years in human resources and 12 as a support worker for people with learning disabilities and challenging behaviour. He published Murdering the Macho Managers in 2019.

REGINALD SUBAROV

Reginald Subarov was born and raised in the United Kingdom. After spending time teaching English in China, he decided to turn his hand to writing, aspiring to publish short and novel-length fiction pieces that cover tales of horror, mystery and survival.

KAROLINA BONDE

Karolina Bonde est d'origine suédoise, elle vit en France. Elle a étudié la littérature à l'Université Américaine de Paris et à NYU. Elle a vendu 27 tableaux au collectionneur Gunther Sachs, ancien mari de Brigitte Bardot. Elle a exposé 3 œuvres avec l'artiste Christo à la galerie Etienne de Causans. www.karolinabonde.com

CÉLINE LOSSOUARN

Céline Lossouarn, née en 1986, réside près de Brest. Sa passion pour l'écriture naît jeune. Diplômée d'une licence en lettres, elle a étudié les langues étrangères et l'audiovisuel. Hôtesse de l'air puis secrétaire, riche de son expérience et son imagination, elle crée le personnage Rosine Delfeuille.

THOMAS RIVERA

Thomas Rivera, d'origine portoricaine et vivant actuellement en Belgique. Né le 12 novembre 1976 dans la municipalité de Coamo sur l'île de Puerto Rico. Malgré des études universitaires médicales, il vogue dans le milieu artistique depuis l'enfance, musique, peinture et écriture. Il envisage en ce moment un retour aux racines.

ZENITRAM

Né en 1984 à Aix en Provence, Didier Martinez «Zenitram», grandit à Gréasque, village entre Aix et Marseille. Passionné de sa région, il s'évertue à lui rendre hommage. Paysages, constructions humaines, saisons, imaginaire et réalité.